LONG HARD FALL

THE WALKER FIVE, BOOK 3

MARIE JOHNSTON

LE PUBLISHING

Long Hard Fall

Cash Walker always leaves a lady's bed before morning—after all, he has a day full of chores waiting on his ranch. So when he wakes up one morning to his latest catch creeping out of the room, he figures he had it coming. Until later the same day, when she shows up in his barn. Turns out, she's come to town to talk about the one subject Cash refuses to discuss with anyone.

Abbi Daniels is tired of being the responsible woman her parents expect her to be, but even she can admit that jumping into bed with the last guy to see her brother alive wasn't her smartest move. Cash won't talk about the day her brother was killed, but she refuses to leave town without answers. Only the more she's around Cash, the less she wants to return home and the more she feels like her old self again.

With Abbi around, Cash's no-commitment resolve breaks down. With Cash, Abbi finds the freedom she's craved for so long. But how will their fragile connection survive when all the things left unsaid between them come to light?

While working on this book, my in-laws planned a family reunion. Instead, we had a funeral.
To the beautiful young soul who left this world too early—you will be forever missed and forever in our hearts.

————————

For new release updates and chapter sneak peeks, sign up for Marie's newsletter via instaFreebie and receive a FREE novella from my Fleet Romance series.

CHAPTER 1

bbi's eyelids fluttered open. Sunlight poured through the drab drapes of her low-end motel room. She inhaled a slow breath and let her lids drift shut again. Her mission in Moore, Minnesota, could wait until she had more rest. It'd been a late night.

Soft inhales and exhales resonated from behind her. Her eyes flew open.

Oh, shit. *Abigail Daniels, what have you done?*

She froze, too afraid to roll over and witness her epically bad decision from the night before.

Think, think, think. She'd come to town with one goal—to find a man. Not just any man, but the one who'd been with her brother when he'd died. But she hadn't started her search. She had reached town, rented a room, and gone out for a bite to eat.

So why was she in bed with a dude who wasn't her boyfriend?

She suppressed a groan and squeezed her eyes shut. That's right. As of yesterday, she was single. Her solid, *respon-*

sible boyfriend had gotten tired of dating a sad sack and argued her trip to Moore was mind-bogglingly impulsive.

Not even her threat of breaking up with him if he couldn't respect how important the trip was had swayed his opinion. And it hadn't been a threat.

There went four years of her life she couldn't get back. Her relationship with Ellis had weathered the death of her brother and her subsequent mourning, but one little trip and Ellis had bailed. Maybe it was for the best. He could be such a downer at times. Most times.

She opened her eyes and stared at the wall, ignoring the stranger slumbering next to her.

What did she remember?

Too much to drink. She was known as an uptight prude in her circle of friends, but that was because they hadn't gone to college with her. Ellis had forbidden her from having more than two drinks because after they'd gotten serious he'd grown tired of holding her hand the next morning when her raging hangover took over. He'd gotten tired of explaining the stupid shit she'd done, too.

But it was college, wasn't that what she was supposed to do?

What was her excuse now?

Her body throbbed in all the right places. Whoever her bedmate was, he must've been satisfying.

Abbi's stomach clenched. No matter how wild she used to be, she wasn't that girl anymore. She'd have to adult the hell out of this.

Steeling herself, she pushed up. It wasn't the first time she'd had to face the morning and piece together the previous night, but it'd been a long time, and it was damn well going to be the last time.

She scanned her body—naked. A few love bites decorated

her breasts. Whatever she'd done with the mystery man had been active. As the fog of sleep faded, she had a hazy memory of a deep voice and a body to die for.

With a gulp, she twisted to look at her hookup.

She was caught between a gasp and a laugh.

Just her luck. She'd hit the jackpot and couldn't recall more than a minute of it.

He was as hot as they came.

Okay, Abbi. You're forgiven for taking him home.

Mussed, sandy-blond hair swept over his forehead, and dark-blond eyelashes rimmed his eyes.

Blue eyes, she remembered. Startlingly blue, and they'd wiped out all thoughts of Ellis when they'd been aimed at her. She remembered that but not his name, dammit.

She bet the sex they'd had was incredible. At least for her. She had enough pride to hope she'd pleased him, too. And pray they'd used protection.

With as much stealth as she could muster, she rolled out of bed. Two condom wrappers lay at her feet.

Good. At least there was that.

But two?

Stretching, her muscles informed her that yes, she'd been pleasured more than once.

No big. She wouldn't let it endear her to the stranger she'd invited into her bed. Even Ellis had given her more than one orgasm in a twenty-four-hour period. A high compliment from a man who feared body fluids and germs as much as he did.

Abbi tiptoed to her luggage and collected fresh clothing. Before she showered, she darted around the room and collected her strewn clothing from the night before. Now all she had to do after she dressed was toss in her toiletry bag and run.

Memories of sultry laughter and wet kisses bombarded her. Eventually, it'd all come back.

She looked forward to it.

The memories would be hers alone. Her last impulsive act before she moved on. She owed it to herself after four years with Ellis.

As long as her family never found out. Wild Child Daniels was forever gone in their minds and she couldn't make a reappearance, no matter how brief. Not after what had happened to her brother. It'd break their hearts if she returned to her partying ways.

Straight-laced Abbi Daniels needed to be the one to return to Green Bay. Her parents were already sick at the thought that she was vacationing alone.

She crept into the bathroom and took the quickest shower of her life. At the sink, she was brushing her teeth and wondering what made up the weird taste in her mouth when she spied a third condom wrapper.

That was it. Alcohol and plastic. God, she hoped he was clean. Even with protection, having her head in the crotch of a man she'd just met wasn't the most hygienic.

Ugh, listen to you. Soon she'd be spouting off STD statistics like Ellis.

She shrugged into her University of Wisconsin-Madison sweatshirt and pulled on her skinny jeans. Her ballet flats had been bundled in her clothing and she pulled them on. Her knee-high boots were packed already, and it would've been too noisy to dig them out. The October days were still warmish so her skimpy shoes would have to do.

Before she opened the door, she ran through her game plan and tried to calm her stomach.

She pushed the door open. The bathroom light fell across the bed. Hotness blinked awake and his crystal-blue gaze landed on her.

For a half a second, she considered abandoning her plan and crawling back into bed with him. Three condom wrappers and a man with his looks… But she couldn't, her family came first. And the reason why she was in Moore sobered her.

Cash stared at the beauty in the doorway. Damp auburn hair, combed and left hanging straight, dripped water spots onto her gray sweatshirt. The red details in the shirt's design only highlighted the green flecks in her wary hazel eyes.

It was her eyes that had attracted him last night. They'd been intelligent and full of laughter, not to mention, she'd been alone and wanting company. Always a good sign for a guy like him, a man who had no wish to string a lady along.

He'd been sure she had a boyfriend, but when he'd asked if she was waiting for someone, she'd shoved out the chair next to her with her foot.

What the hell was he still doing in her room? He never slept over. It gave women the wrong idea, and even if he wanted some morning action, he had chores on his ranch to do.

He squinted at the window where sunlight streamed in around the curtains.

Chores he was late for. Hungry horses waited for him, and Patsy Cline could be a hangry beast.

And it'd still be a late night helping his cousins man the combines for harvest.

He swung his gaze back to the woman who looked primed to bolt.

Abbi. No last name. What a coincidence. He hadn't given her his, either.

"Mornin'." His voice was rough from sleep.

"So, um…" She shifted her weight and adjusted the small polka-dot bag in her hands. "Take your time. I think checkout is eleven or something."

She sidled to her suitcase and zipped her bag inside.

"You're leaving?" He tried to sound cool, but it came out incredulous.

Some of the best sex of his life and *she* was ditching *him*.

The irony.

"Yeah, sorry. I've gotta go…stuff to do." She hefted her bag and gave the room a once-over before she, reluctantly, met his gaze.

He sat up, the blankets slipping off his torso. Her bright gaze dipped to his chest. Pink lips parted and heat flared in her lovely eyes. He couldn't help his smug grin.

Three orgasms and she was still primed for him.

She noticed his smile. Her back went ramrod straight. False bravado?

"Thanks for the, uh…thanks for the good time." She winced and scurried for the door.

He wanted to chuckle at her awkwardness. As she was leaving, he called, "Nice to meet you, Abbi."

Her shoulders stiffened. She glanced back with a flash of regret in her eyes. "Same here."

The door closed over her fine ass. He stared at the scuffed metal.

So it was like that, huh?

He scratched his head. He must look as rumpled as he felt.

He blew out a breath and studied the room. Had he been in this one before? Sometimes he brought his hookups to one of the motels in town. Anywhere but home was his rule. Can't sneak out of his own house because they'd still be there when he came back in from chores. And some girls would never leave. Sometimes, if he hooked up with a girl more than once, she'd start thinking along the lines of a relation-ship. But they hadn't grown up in his house, with his parents' shining example.

Cash shuddered. No thanks.

Relationships weren't for him, but he had to admit, getting ditched by his fling stung.

He rubbed his chest. That didn't bother him, did it? It couldn't. He'd only met her—he glanced at the time—twelve hours ago.

Dang, he had to get home. He and his cousins would be pulling the cattle off the pastures soon and he had some fencing to reinforce before that happened.

Groaning, he pushed himself up. Sitting on the edge of the bed, he scrubbed his face. Had he fallen asleep? With a stranger?

Maybe it made sense. He'd always slept fine in the barracks in the army. After that last deployment, well, night-mares could be worse than what had gone on over there.

No. He yanked himself out of the self-pity sinkhole. His few nights of disrupted sleep were better than the family that'd lost their son and brother.

Still, it'd be worth a second round with Abbi just to get another night of uninterrupted sleep. He started getting dressed.

There was a knock on the door. A feminine voice called "housekeeping" a millisecond before the door opened. A young girl's eyes went wide at the sight of him buttoning his pants. Thank goodness he'd gotten that far.

"I-I'm sorry," she stuttered. "I thought no one was in here."

"Give a guy a few minutes before busting the door open," he drawled with a good-natured smile.

Her stare was stuck on his naked abdomen and it changed

from shocked to interested. Lord, she was barely old enough to vote.

"Kiddo," he said, "I'll clear on out of here in a few minutes, then the room is all yours."

She pushed the door open a little farther and attempted to strike a provocative pose. His heart sank at the sight. All he saw was his sister standing there before all the bad decisions she'd made, especially the ones following in his footsteps.

"Do me a favor?" he asked and her face lit up. "Don't ever date a guy a like me."

She frowned and her gaze landed back on his abs. "Why?"

"I don't treat women right, and you should never put up with someone like me." Aside from him being a good ten years older than her.

"Is that why your girlfriend left?"

"Yes, because I'm a waste of time." The words rang too true. But he'd rather be honest than make a woman as miserable as his dad made his mom.

The girl rolled her eyes and stepped out. "Whatever." Said with all the attitude a girl her age could muster.

He finished dressing and found his pickup where Abbi had directed him to park it last night. The spot next to his was empty. Abbi was done and gone.

Where had she said she was from again?

Oh, yeah, she hadn't.

His mouth quirked. He'd wanted to get to know her. Not too much new meat came to town, but she'd been…different. Sweet. The other girls he "dated" were sweet, too, but Abbi was…different. It was like she hadn't cared if Cash hit on her or not, but she'd been delighted to just laugh and joke around. Even more delighted when he'd accepted her overt invitation back to her room. A guy could get used to that level of comfort with a girl.

No thinking along those lines. He'd been ditched, and he was man enough to take it since he'd dished it out plenty of times before.

$\mathcal{A}$bbi set her items on the gas station counter and assessed the cashier. If anyone knew everyone in town, it'd be the bespectacled, gray-haired lady manning the cash register. "I'm looking for Reno Walker."

"Who?" The cashier's incredulous expression would be embarrassing if Abbi's head wasn't pounding.

"Reno Walker."

The woman shook her head. "There is no one in town named Reno, I can guarantee, but we've got a ton of Walker boys. Maybe you're looking for one of them?"

"Maybe. My brother always called him Reno. They were in the army together."

An older guy waiting in line behind her spoke up. "A couple of the young Walkers were in the army. Maybe it's one of them."

The clerk rang up Abbi's pathetic breakfast of a chocolate-glazed pastry and diet soda. She'd started off the morning very un-Abbi-like, or rather, more Abbi-like than she'd wanted. Why not revert to another college habit? She just hoped it stayed down.

The woman rattled off the price before saying, "That's right, a couple of them were. George, why don't you give her directions to the Walker spread. They'll help her out."

Abbi handed over her cash while the poster-child for an old farmer with his denim overalls and dirty trucker's hat rattled off things like "turn north" and "head west." All Abbi got from the conversation was that there were five Walker cousins who farmed and ranched and they all lived around each other. Moore was small; how hard would it be to find them?

She drove for a couple of hours with no luck. She now knew Moore by heart and every avenue in and out of town. Finally, she stopped at another gas station where a man about her age was more than willing to help her with directions. A greasy hot dog somehow called her name, and she grabbed another soda. And a water so she could claim one responsible thing for the morning.

After receiving the most thorough directions of her life, and getting warned about one particular Walker named Cash who was a heartbreaker, she was on the highway and pointing in the right direction. She munched on her food and drained her soda. Breakfast had stayed down so she'd taken it as a good sign, despite her stomach's constant upset.

She cruised past her turnoff. "Oh, shit." Time to find an approach to turn around.

Straight shot on gravel, the man had said.

She drove for a mile or two and wouldn't have minded a few more. The countryside was gorgeous. Brightly colored leaves still decorated the trees, and golden or already harvested fields surrounded her. The temps were supposed to be moderate today, and she would have loved to dig out her athletic shoes and taken a nature hike if she'd felt better.

Two houses—more like the trees surrounding the houses —came into view. The place on her left was concealed by a few rows of trees, but the place on her right was only partially blocked from view.

Which one should she choose? She slowed to a stop since no one else was on the road. The man who'd warned her of Cash Walker had said he lived… Dammit, she couldn't remember. There goes her scatterbrain, as Ellis always said. She rolled her eyes at herself like she would've at him.

She picked the house on the right that didn't have as many trees. It was more sensible to approach strange men out in the open.

Her parents would die eighty deaths if they knew what she was up to. Ellis was supposed to have accompanied her, but he'd had a shit-fit. Didn't stop her, though. Her family had only gotten vague stories about her brother's death, and she wanted closure. Needed it. She couldn't be Responsible Abbi when her mind hounded her for answers. Something deep inside drove her to seek out her brother's old army buddies, and if that meant knocking on the doors of random farmers, so be it. She'd find Reno Walker from Moore, Minnesota, and she'd get the full rundown of how her brother had died.

She turned into the drive. At first glance, the yard appeared cluttered, but it was actually neatly fenced off. Pens and corrals ran parallel to the road. Stacks of hay three bales high rimmed one edge of the property. A long barn separated the pens from the yard. Another huge barn also had fences coming off it and horses meandered around inside.

Parking in front of the house, she didn't get out and it wasn't because her food threatened to heave. She was looking at the cutest old farmhouse she'd ever seen; not even her grandparents' house had been as adorable. Two stories high, painted white with yellow shutters, it was picturesque, but it was the wraparound porch that Abbi would kill for. Any direction, point your rocking chair and chill. Fantasies of sketching the horizon while the sun set dominated her thoughts. Summer nights would be divine.

How long since she'd sketched? Since they'd received the dreaded knock on the door announcing Perry's death.

She climbed out and expected to be hit with the smell of manure, but fresh country air was all that greeted her.

Her breath hitched. This was it. Her first step on her hunt for Reno.

She knocked on the door. And waited. And waited. Knocked again. Rang the doorbell. Nothing.

Frowning, she pivoted and scanned the yard.

An obnoxiously large pickup sat outside the long barn. Must be the thing for the guys around here. She had a vague recollection of climbing into a truck just as big last night. Knowing she'd be in no shape to drive, she'd chosen a place close enough to walk, totally not planning on hooking a ride back. She pushed the thought away. Her hot hookup would only distract her.

A horse whinnied. Was someone down there?

She eyeballed her shoes. Should she dig out her boots? Well, it wasn't like she was going tromping through manure. She just had to flag someone down to let them know she was here and wanted to talk.

Nimbly, she picked her way over the gravel driveway that led to the barn.

The deep rumble of a man's voice and a horse's answering whinny sounded deep inside the barn. Straw littered the floor; she chose her steps carefully. The far barn door was open and she spied movement.

Peeking around the corner, she was impressed by the sight.

"Whoa, Patsy Cline. Calm down, girl." A man with surprisingly broad shoulders sat astride a massive brown horse. His back was to her with the sun blazing behind him, so she couldn't distinguish specific features other than an amazing body and voice. She shaded her eyes, but her headache roared back to do an I-told-you-so that she should've drunk more water.

God, that voice. Yummier than the one she remembered from last night. Or the one she heard in her hangover-fogged state this morning. But she wasn't running out on this guy. To get the information she needed, she'd be staying to chat for a while.

The horse's rear end swung to the side and it shook its big head while the mesmerizing guy murmured encouraging words.

She didn't know if this was a bad time, but she knocked lightly. The sound didn't carry over the horse's scratching hooves.

She knocked louder and the man's head whipped around. She was nailed with a vivid blue gaze.

Her stomach plummeted and her mouth dropped open. She squeaked.

Oh. My. God.

No.

∼

A slow grin spread across his face. "Well, well. We meet again."

Her mouth hung open while she gaped at him. Ordinarily, if a girl stalked him home, he'd be panicking, but the look on Abbi's face was too filled with horror.

He swiveled Patsy Cline around and patted her neck. "Good girl." But he didn't take his eyes off Abbi. Didn't want to. In the dim motel room, she was *smokin'*, but her ethereal beauty was enhanced in the light of day. Her hair had dried and hung in soft waves around a face that'd gone pale.

Her mouth snapped shut. She frantically looked around, as if searching for anyone else to talk to. One hand flew to her lips and the other to her abdomen. Then she abruptly turned into the barn and heaved.

Cash's brows flew up. Patsy Cline shifted underneath him, sensing the disturbance. He dismounted and tied her off on the side of the corral. He stole a second to soothe his horse before he checked on the sick woman.

Horrible retching came from Abbi as she lost the contents of her stomach. He rushed to her side and ignored the mess at her feet, more concerned about her being ill than having muck to clean.

"Oh my god, I am so sorry." She wiped her mouth on her sleeve and a blush stained her cheeks. At least she'd gotten some color back.

"I'll throw some straw on it and shovel it out. No need to worry. Are you feeling okay?"

She nodded, then winced. "Too much to drink last night."

What? "Honey, you didn't seem that bad off, and you only had a couple beers while we were chatting." Before she'd beckoned him back to her room, where he'd burned through his stash of condoms.

"I had a few before you showed up." She buried her head in her hands and backed away from the spew on the ground. "And a couple of shots before supper."

"Whoa." He used the same tone he had used on his horse. Abbi's gaze darted all over like she was about to flee. "I swear, if I'd thought you were wasted, I wouldn't have taken you up on your offer."

It'd have killed him to miss out on her banging body, but he was into fully conscious partners only.

She waved him off. "Not your fault. I hold my alcohol well. Until I don't. I…gotta go."

She was getting away from him. Again. When she stumbled slightly, he swooped in to pick her up.

"Oh." She pushed at his chest, her expression full of dismay. "Don't do that. I stink."

He smiled in reassurance. Vomit smell or not, it didn't decrease her appeal. "I'll take you to the house and you can clean up while I get my mare settled." Worry plagued him. Patsy Cline wasn't acting right, but he needed to take care of Abbi first. "Then you can tell me why you're here."

She relaxed into him like she had when they'd been alone in her room. He'd been reliving it all freaking morning.

He aimed straight for his house, juggled her while finagling the handle, and nudged the door open with his boot. Abbi's color was stabilizing, her healthy glow returning.

Settling her on the couch, he said, "Use what you need; I'll be right back."

The burn of her eyes licked his back as he walked out the way he'd come. Why did he have to be so aware of her?

He gauged the time. The horses had been fed and the section fence repaired. He should be meeting up with Dillon to give him a break from the combine. Patsy Cline had delayed him when he'd noticed she wasn't interested in her food and was pawing at the ground. He'd been trying to get her back into the stall to monitor her symptoms when Abbi had interrupted.

He jogged to the barn and unhooked his horse. She was whinnying and pawing hard. He managed to get the suffering horse into a stall before she decided to drop and roll.

Hell, that was a bad sign. Withdrawing his phone, he hit speed dial. "Hey, Doc, it's Patsy Cline."

He rattled off the symptoms and hung up. Torn between

his sick horse and a sick Abbi, he sighed. Doc would take care of Patsy Cline; he'd have to take care of Abbi.

On his way back to the house, he texted Dillon about the colic and the vet but didn't mention the woman on his couch. When he got inside, the couch was empty. Sounds of splashing water came from the small bathroom in the narrow hallway.

He was used to entertaining his cousins but was at a loss for what to do in this situation. He stared at his boots for a few moments, trying to come up with something to do while waiting.

Water.

He went into the kitchen to pour a glass of water. Coming back into the living room, his steps loud on the hardwood, he heard the bathroom door squeak open. Abbi couldn't sneak away in this old house.

"I have some water for you." He set it on the end table.

Abbi scooted around him and settled on the edge of the couch with her small suitcase at her feet. She must've grabbed it while he'd been wrestling with his horse. Her sweatshirt this time was a black hoodie with neon trim. Yoga pants showed off her legs, and athletic shoes capped off the look. Sporty was the only style he'd seen her in, but she did it well.

Her face pinched. "I'm so sorry about the barn."

"Don't worry. Pull out a few calves stuck in the birth canal and puke won't bother you."

Her lips curled in disgust. "Uck, I'll pass. But it's still embarrassing."

He had so many questions. *Why'd you leave this morning? Why'd you invite me back for some fun between the sheets in the first place?* But he started with the most pressing. "So, what are you doing out here? Did you get lost?"

She shook her head. "No, I came to Moore looking for one of my brother's friends. Two, actually."

"Did they leave you hanging at the bar last night?"

Several expressions traveled across her lovely features. "No, I was…drowning my sorrows, you could say. I planned to go searching today and—" she spread her hands, "—here I am."

He reclined against the wall with his arms crossed. She hadn't seemed sad last night. "And your search brought you to me. Who's your brother?"

"Yeah, I need directions to the guys my brother served with. My brother's name was Perry Daniels."

CHAPTER 3

His expression went blank. Dammit, why couldn't she remember his name? Had she screamed it at some point last night? The more she was around him, the more flashes of memory she experienced. Especially when she'd been cradled against his strong chest. Lots of naked images had bombarded her mind then.

She wanted more.

But she was here for a much different reason. "I know only one guy's full name, but their last name is Walker. No one I've talked to knows who Reno Walker is, but they said the Walkers live out this way." Why hadn't she asked him last night how she could find Reno Walker? Because she'd been medicating her anger with copious amounts of alcohol. And then he'd taken her mind off…everything. "So, I guess I'll ask you. Do you know who Reno is?"

He shifted his stance and briefly looked away. He swallowed hard.

"You aren't Reno, are you?" She kept her tone hopeful over the dread crawling its way up her throat. Why was he acting like he didn't want to tell her?

He lost the strange expression and shot her a forced smile. "You know my name."

Her face must've revealed her alarm because he looked away and shook his head. A muscle in his jaw tensed and relaxed.

"You don't remember."

"It's coming back, slowly." Probably as much as it ever would.

"You were blackout drunk?"

"No." Kinda.

His look said he didn't believe her. "Are you even okay to be driving yet?"

"I get a little sick when I drink and I'm paying for it." Oh god, had she slept off enough before she'd rushed out of the hotel room? She hadn't been dizzy, but that wasn't the best estimate of intoxication. "Now, can we get back to Reno? Where can I find him?"

He swung his empty stare down the hallway for a few heartbeats. "You found him."

She glanced around, like a new dude would suddenly appear. But it was just her handsome hookup.

"*You're* Reno?" Oh. Oh hell. Only she would have the misfortune to pick up her brother's friend. Her epic episode of irresponsibility had just reached new heights.

What would Perry have thought? He hadn't been a fan of Ellis, but to run right into his buddy's arms…

"That's a name I haven't heard in a long time. It was my nickname. I'm Cash, by the way." His bitter tone wasn't lost on her.

Cash. Double hell. The only man she'd ever been warned away from and she'd picked him up first.

Cash Walker was Reno Walker. Elation replaced mortification.

"I found you," she breathed. It couldn't be this easy,

could it? She wouldn't have to scour the town. It was unfortunate she'd picked him up at the bar, but here they were.

He shoved his hands into his pockets and turned to glower out the large picture window. "You found me all right."

Was that resentment? She didn't care; she couldn't care.

"Why did my brother call you Reno?"

He glanced over his shoulder, his eyes nearly glowing from the sunshine. He hadn't taken his hat off, but the blue of his irises radiated from under the brim. If he smiled, he'd probably devastate whoever he aimed it at. No wonder she'd been warned off. He probably galloped through women's beds.

"Because I get lucky all the time."

Nailed it. But he didn't sound proud.

"And because my cousin was a team leader in the same platoon, so it was how the guys kept us straight," he finished. "And because we were stationed together for the last four years, which probably had worse odds of happening than winning the lotto. They just thought I was all around lucky I guess."

"Did you two get out of the army after…after, uh…" Unbidden tears sprang up and she hastily wiped them away. This wasn't how she'd pictured it all going. Throwing up in the man's barn, then barely being able to speak when she tried to talk about what she'd come here for.

"Yeah." His voice was thick. "Dillon and I enlisted at the same time, so we got out at the same time."

She nodded woodenly. He stood quietly. She ran her hand along the fabric of the couch, the smooth texture doing nothing to lull her conflicted emotions.

"You're Daniels's little sis, huh."

"Yep." Now that she was here, she was at a loss for what to

do. She couldn't just blurt out the question that had been haunting her. "Are you and your cousin doing okay?"

His broad shoulders tightened in his long sleeve shirt. "Yeah, we're fine. Work keeps us busy, and I'll take slinging cows around over humping seventy pounds of equipment through the desert any day."

"Perry said he hated all the sand and heat, wished he'd never gone into the infantry."

Cash grunted. "That makes two of us."

"What happened?" Oops. She'd blurted it anyway.

He sighed and faced her. "Didn't they tell you?"

"They told me you guys were clearing a building and he set off an IED."

"Then you know what happened."

"Do I?"

"I don't know what you're looking for, Abbi. I'm sorry. I relive it—"

A honk from outside cut him off.

"That's the vet. I gotta go out and meet her." He charged out the door. Abbi jumped up to chase after him. She was finally digging into what she was here for, and he was running away.

A cute woman who looked way too short to drive the size of pickup she did hopped down and greeted Cash with a big smile. He walked toward her with his arms wide, and the woman laughed and jumped into them.

Abbi refused to be jealous, especially after she'd run from a naked Cash hours ago. But she increased her pace out of curiosity.

The woman pounded Cash heartily on the back before releasing him. She was older than Abbi had previously thought. Somewhere in her thirties, but her curves couldn't be denied. When her gaze landed on Abbi, she cut off mid-sentence.

Cash glanced at Abbi, exasperation in his eyes. "Doc, this is Abbi, the sister of an old army buddy. Abbi, this is Dr. Bonita Wilson."

The vet's expression grew serious and speculative. She stuck her hand out. "Nice to meet you. Just call me Bunny. I'll even forgive you a giggle about the irony of a vet named Bunny."

Abbi couldn't help her smile as she shook hands.

Bunny switched her attention to Cash. "You said it was Patsy Cline. Afraid she has colic again?"

"I tried to ride her, but she wasn't acting right. I hadn't noticed when I was feeding her, but I should've." He gave Abbi a sidelong look. "I was distracted."

Bunny grinned and wiggled her brows as she turned to head to the barn.

Abbi kept up with them and crossed her fingers that her vomit mess had been cleaned away. She suppressed a sigh of relief. Cash had been true to his word.

"Oh my, poor girl." Bunny crooned and comforted the horse as she inspected her.

Abbi jumped when Cash's hot breath wafted over her earlobe. "You don't have to wait here. This might take a while."

The man could move with stealth. "I don't mind. Or am I interrupting something?" Had that come out catty?

"You aren't interrupting a thing," Bunny piped up from in the stall. "He can tell you about all the times I almost swatted his bottom at the pranks he pulled."

Cash chuckled and the low sound gave Abbi shivers. Oh yeah, there was another memory of last night.

"It was Mom's fault for putting you in charge of me and Sissy when you were only six years older."

"I didn't even get paid. Your mom thought since I was

family I should work for free. Those rules no longer apply, by the way." Bunny went back to work.

"Doc is my second cousin. Our grams are sisters." Cash opened the stall to enter. "Hey, uh, I can call you later if you want to go back into town. This might take a while, and I doubt your stomach will tolerate it."

"I can wait."

"Abbi." Cash draped his arms over the stall gate to watch the exam. Hoof scrapes and horse grunts came from inside with Bunny muttering encouraging words. "I've got a long day. My horse is sick and we're in the middle of harvest. Dillon has been in a combine for hours already and we need to work until sundown. I was supposed to be taking over for him now, but I'm here."

She tried to keep her expression pleasant, but it probably teetered toward droll. "And are you really going to call?"

"I said I would."

"How many girls have you told that to?"

Bunny snorted. Cash clamped his mouth shut.

"Exactly." Abbi pushed her hair back. "Why don't we plan a time to meet?" Her cheeks warmed. Would he think she had plans to hit on him again?

"My day tomorrow is exactly like today. Without a dead horse, I hope."

The concern in his features was endearing. He was worried about Patsy Cline. Abbi hoped she recovered, but she couldn't let Cash squirm out of talking to her.

"You gotta eat, Cash. Come on. I need to talk to you." She got the sentence out before she choked back a sob. An unknown someone picked that time to ring her. Between her phone and her insistent tears, she had to leave. No answers today.

She mustered a smile despite her disappointment and was turning away to answer the call when Cash spoke.

Distress glimmered in his eyes and he looked away. "All right. Meet me out here for lunch tomorrow before I trade with Dillon."

Nodding, afraid he'd change his mind, she nearly ran back to her car while digging her phone out.

Her parents were going to call her every damn day, weren't they?

She checked the screen.

Even worse. Ellis. So not what she needed. Did she have to answer? She debated until right before her voicemail kicked in.

She answered in a bored voice, "Moore Sewage Treatment. How may I direct your call?"

Silence greeted her.

Finally, Ellis spoke. "You're cracking jokes after the way we parted?"

"What do you want, Ellis?" She couldn't muster the energy to be angry, but his authoritative attitude rankled. How had she not noticed it before?

"I'm checking to see how you're doing."

Not as simple a question as he probably thought. *I got drunk last night and took the best-looking piece of ass home. I don't remember much, but I know it was goooood.* "I'm fine."

"Have you found Reno Walker?"

Had she ever. "He's going to talk to me later."

"Maybe I should come up there."

Distress choked off her mental *No!* Yesterday, she'd drunk too much because he hadn't come with her. Now, him being here sounded like the worst idea in history. "Why? We're not together anymore."

"I care about you, Abigail."

Abigail. So grown up. So proper. So how he wanted her.

"I'm fine, Ellis, but I have to go."

He started speaking, but she made static sounds and hung up. How immature.

God that felt good.

~

Cash resisted the urge to jump out of the stall and watch Abbi saunter away. Then he resisted the urge to jump out of the stall and watch Abbi drive away. Either way, she was leaving and it was a giant relief with a gaping hole of regret.

Perry Daniels's little sister.

He could've gone his whole life without meeting her. The wild little sister Daniels had worried about. Cash hadn't lied; he'd told her what had really happened. They'd been clearing a building and her brother hadn't walked out alive with the rest of them. He almost hadn't, either, thanks to Daniels.

His eyes drifted shut. He'd slept with Daniels's little sister. He couldn't save the man and then he'd bedded his sister.

"You with me, cuz?"

He started and covered it by stroking Patsy Cline. Worry overrode his tumultuous feelings—barely.

"I caught her early enough, tell me I did, Doc." If he'd left Abbi after sex like his standard MO, he would've been up early like usual and might've noticed his mare's condition then. In his haste, he'd missed the warning signs of colic.

"Now that your company's gone, I'll do the rectal exam. If that's clear, all she'll need is to be tubed to let the gas out."

Cash assisted his cousin. Being around horses his whole life, and with a cousin who let him glove up and help, he was familiar with the process. What he wasn't prepared for was losing his girl. Patsy Cline was one of his first major purchases, even before he'd taken over the ranching side of the Walker Five operation. He and the colic-prone mare had bonded, and horse therapy was legit. Just not enough to fix his issues.

With the pressure eased on the creature and Bunny's promise to check on her later so he could relieve Dillon, Cash went to his house to clean up.

Popping in through the front door, he did his damnedest to ignore Abbi's lingering floral scent. His body stirred, and he ruthlessly tamped it down. No more drinking from that trough.

On the way to the same tiny bathroom she had used, he scanned his walls. Had she stopped and looked at his family photos? Had she noticed his mom and dad were rarely in the same one?

For reasons only obvious to him and his sister, his parents hadn't wanted their turbulent marriage immortalized.

Nah. Why would Abbi pay attention to any of that? She'd made it clear when she'd sprinted out of the motel room that she wasn't here for anything beyond her brother's story.

Cash shook his head. Typical Daniels. Sticking him with the fallout.

He freshened up and hopped into his truck to go in search of Dillon. Cash chose an approach that bordered the field Dillon was harvesting and parked. Exiting his pickup, he texted Dillon and dropped the tailgate to have a seat.

The trees of the shelter belts were losing their leaves but wouldn't be bare until the temps dropped closer to freezing day after day. More wind got through them in the fall, but they still proved to be nature's snow fence when necessary.

The soy field looked like it'd seen better days, but to a farmer like him, it looked like dollar signs. They were grateful for the harvest, especially after a nasty hail storm in July had taken out significant portions of their crop. Despite the afternoon chill, the sun was warm and shining bright. Cash tipped his face up to it and cursed.

Flashing hazel eyes and a saucy grin filled his head. Why couldn't he quit thinking about Abbi? Perhaps he'd known deep down that they had an ominous connection.

Yeah, that was it. It had nothing to do with how her body had not only felt like paradise, but with how uninhibited she'd been.

He ground his teeth. But she'd been fucking drunk. Her reaction hadn't been real.

Abbi Daniels. He took off his hat and cradled his head in his hands, elbows on his knees. He couldn't forget her, and all the while she couldn't remember him.

CHAPTER 4

Dillon had already made two rounds on the quarter of land that comprised the field. The magnificent red combine came into view as the drone of the engine reached Cash. Dread built about the upcoming conversation with his cousin. They'd just reached a solid point in their bro-ship after years of Dillon blaming Cash's irresponsible side for Daniels's death. Cash was always responsible when it counted.

He slid onto the tailgate, waiting for Dillon to pause the operation and swap duties.

The combine rumbled to a stop. Dillon scaled down from the cab and jogged toward him. He carried his lunch pail and nimbly picked through piles of shredded soybean plants.

Dillon reached him barely out of breath. "How's Patsy Cline?"

He got a run in almost every morning, while Cash only met him two or three times a week, just like old times in the army. They'd pass for brothers with the same body frames and similar features. Only Dillon's rusty brown hair was obviously different compared to Cash's sandy blond. Cash was only a month younger, and they'd been inseparable their whole lives—they might as well be twins. Admittedly, in their army days, they may have claimed to be twins once or twice to women.

"What's wrong?" Dillon's clear gaze was concerned. Cash's chest grew heavy.

Only six months ago, he'd been afraid Dillon was going to crawl into a bottle and screw on the lid. Now, he was bright eyed and bushy tailed, with a smart and intelligent woman waiting for him at home. Figuratively only. Elle did her own thing and Dillon gladly chased after her. But Dillon's parents had been like that until the death of his dad. Cash's heart broke for his Aunt Christy, but the anticipation of grandkids in her future seemed to keep a spring in her step. If Cash couldn't have any of that in his life, at least he got to witness it with Dillon.

"I got a visitor today," Cash said. Oh *fuck*. Telling Dillon about Abbi was bad enough, but he might as well come clean about how they'd met. As if anyone needed more proof that he was a poster child for commitment phobia. "Let me start at the beginning. I met a woman last night."

Dillon snorted and Cash scowled at him.

"This one left me in the dust."

"Seriously?" Dillon's surprised tone matched what Cash had felt watching Abbi walk out the door.

"Yeah. Ran out as soon as she woke, but here's the thing." Cash drew in a weighted breath and blew it out. "She shows up again at my place looking for Reno Walker."

"*What?* Wait, she didn't know you were Reno when you two…"

"Nope." *Didn't even remember my name.* "And we didn't swap last names. You know how it goes." Cash smiled easily. "If your memory goes back that far."

The corner of Dillon's mouth lifted, but he remained serious, waiting for the bad news.

"Yeah, so," Cash said gruffly, "she introduced herself as Abbi Daniels."

Color leeched from Dillon's face. Cash had known what was coming, but his heart rate sped up anyway.

"Damn, Cash. What's she doing in Moore?"

"Looking for us—me. Mostly me. Thinks she didn't get the whole story behind her brother's death."

Dillon's head tipped back.

"Yeah."

Dillon took his hat off and shoved a hand through his hair. "What'd you tell her?"

"I asked her what she'd been told. She knew we'd been clearing a building and he'd set off an IED. But she didn't seem to believe me when I said that was it."

His cousin's mouth twisted. "I hope you were a little gentler than that."

"Of course. I'm not an ass."

Dillon grunted. "Not at all." Cash flipped him off. Dillon shooed him over on the tailgate and settled down next to him. "She's looking for closure then."

"She won't find it with me. What am I going to say? 'Your brother was kind of a flake and died because he didn't listen to orders'?"

"Maybe she heard mutterings when they went through all his paperwork with the army. What are you going to tell her?"

"You know I can't say anything. I'm not going to be responsible for tarnishing the image of her big bro. And as for the other…I'm not going there. It wasn't my business."

"The hell it wasn't. It almost got you killed with him."

"But it didn't." The day replayed in front of Cash's eyes. Searing-hot temperatures. Sand in his eyes, his gear, clogging his pores. Yelling at Daniels to leave. The guy looking at him, looking away, and purposely charging into that room. A dull throb settled in Cash's temples. Great. A long afternoon by himself in an enclosed space with nothing but memories, remorse, and guilt. "If I go saying shit like that, what if it causes a rift in the family?"

"No. I agree. There's honesty and there's hurting his family."

They fell quiet, both of them staring at the red combine.

"You doing okay?" Dillon asked quietly.

Good question. After his talk, he planned to call Bunny. If he lost Patsy Cline on top of getting his emotional Band-Aid ripped off, it'd be a shitty few weeks. "Peachy. You?"

"Brings up some memories I'd rather forget, but it's not like they leave anyway."

"She might want to talk to you, too." She might get distraught, and he didn't like thinking of that. The easy laughter they'd shared over drinks shouldn't be dulled.

They'd joked and chatted about everything from the food at the bar and grill to the cantankerous hotel owner who'd offered to introduce her to his grandson. Cash had gone to school with him and had regaled her with stories of their pranks. No personal topics had been touched on. Cash was an expert at that and she hadn't seemed to mind.

The smile had been wiped off her face this morning and he missed it.

"I don't mind meeting with her, if it'll make her feel better," Dillon said. "It's the least I can do. I'll always feel a little responsible."

And Cash would always feel a whole lot responsible. The situation with Abbi had taken up way too much time this morning.

"Well," Cash jumped off the tailgate, "the beans ain't gonna thrash themselves."

"Cash…"

He called over his shoulder. "Go home, clean up, spend some time with Elle."

Dillon took care of everyone else first. Cash didn't want to be the curse on another relationship.

Seriously, Abigail.

She scowled at her phone as she sat cross-legged on her bed in her hotel room. Ellis had texted the message after she'd hung up on him.

He chastised her behavior and he wasn't even here. Why did he always think he was the measuring stick that everything should be compared to?

How had she tolerated it?

The answer came quickly. Her parents. They liked him so much, and they'd liked the change in her when she'd started dating him.

Abbi had liked Ellis and how grounded he'd made her feel. She was honest enough with herself to know she'd been growing out of control. Her partying was going to hurt her one day, and she'd needed to grow up.

So she'd settled into a relationship with the new man in her life. He'd accompanied her everywhere, probably because he didn't trust her. The drinks and laughter would flow while he glowered at her and hinted it was time to get home. After a year of dating, her wild child was put into the corner for a timeout. She hadn't seen near as much of her friends, and she and Ellis had spent all their time together.

Abbi recalled those suffocating days and the moment she'd resolved to break it off. She had just graduated from college and Ellis had "surprised" her with an apartment to move into together.

Living with Ellis. The idea had crashed reality down hard. Live the rest of her life feeling suppressed and under constant scrutiny? Nope. It had been time to break up with her handler.

Then her parents had called, and life had stopped on a dime.

Perry was gone.

Abbi blinked away tears. God, she still missed him. He hadn't liked Ellis, thought he was too pretentious and had noticed Abbi wasn't as happy as she used to be.

"He's not right for you, Abs," Perry had said after he'd met Ellis.

Oh, but her parents had loved him and how could Abbi shove Ellis away from them after they'd lost Perry?

The next three years hadn't been bad. She'd been too devastated to care about what anyone thought, and she'd begrudgingly admit that Ellis had been a huge support. Too much time had lapsed and Ellis's support had turned into a crutch. The longer she leaned on him, the more he thought she couldn't adequately function without him.

But she'd been coming out of her fog, pushing back against Ellis and his wishes more and more. The weekend she'd spent going through Perry's belongings before she'd decided on a trip to Moore had been more than cathartic. It'd brought up all the questions her parents had had over the years. The ones that had gone unanswered. No one from Perry's old unit had ever stopped by to talk to them, having said their good-byes before Perry's body came home.

A tear dripped onto her phone and she wiped it away.

Seriously, Abigail.

As serious as death, Ellis, she finally texted back.

She wanted to talk to the men Perry had been the closest to. Wanted to know if Perry had known his family loved and missed him. Wanted to know how Perry had been. He hadn't sounded like her jovial brother the few times she'd gotten to talk on the phone with him when he was over there. His letters and emails had grown shorter and shorter and hinted at despondence.

Then the last phone call, he'd been Perry again. Told her to be true to herself. She'd asked him what that meant.

"Come on, Abs. You've become boring as fuck. Lose the jackass and have some fun. It's all going to be all right."

It's all going to be all right.

It hadn't been since then.

She glanced at the time. She had an hour before she had to meet Cash. Flutters tickled her belly.

Looking forward to seeing him again? No, just relieved to be able to talk about her brother and that was it. Had to be. She couldn't sniff around Cash for anything more. *Hey, Mom and Dad, not only did I meet this guy as a random hookup, but he's Perry's friend. You know, one of the ones that ignored us after he died?*

Perry hadn't been close to many men he was deployed with, complained it was hard to meet a woman when he chose a male-dominated field like infantry. But he'd gushed about the Walkers.

Abbi groaned and flopped back. Another memory of chatting with Perry tugged at her.

"Reno's awesome, Abbi, the exact opposite of Ellis. You need to find a guy somewhere in between. Not Reno, not Ellis, but a normal guy who'll treat you right, one that's Perry-approved."

She'd been warned off Cash before she'd even known him. Then she'd been warned off him again when she'd gotten to town. And who had landed in her bed? And who made her insides molten when she thought of having lunch with him?

She groaned and rolled over. Her first instinct was to hit her makeup and do her hair, but she talked herself down. She wasn't as worried about presentation as Ellis, no longer had to be the poster child for his growing financial advisor business.

But she had some pride. She pushed herself up and went to the bathroom. Throwing her hair up into a ponytail, she evaluated her outfit. Black athletic leggings and a running sweater with neon piping. Ironically, she'd thrown it on after her run earlier this morning.

This little vacation was earning its worth just being able to hang out in comfortable clothing all day. Her business-casual attire from work didn't suit her—itchy slacks and tops that she had to race to remove from the dryer or she'd have to drag out the dreaded iron. On vacation, she didn't have to worry about taking a flat iron to her hair, or stiff clothes, or even makeup.

No oatmeal for breakfast, either. Typical Abbi, she was usually running late so Ellis always made them breakfast. She didn't have anything against oatmeal, but after the hundredth morning in a row, a girl got desperate. Not desperate enough to wake up earlier, though, so she'd shovel in her oats while praying someone brought goodies to work.

What would Cash serve for lunch?

She'd be early if she left now, but sitting in her room and reminiscing was killing her.

Her phone pinged.

I'll call after work. Don't play games.

Games. That's all Ellis thought this was. That she'd run home and shrink under the pressure of finding her own place and she'd default to their relationship. When he didn't get his way with her, he made it her fault. She'd capitulated so often that she barely noticed how she constantly took the easy route to avoid conflict.

When she'd left town, she'd finally stood her ground.

"I don't think it's a good idea, Abigail. You go through your

brother's things and decide you have to find his friends. Ones your parents were deeply hurt by. Now you're packed and leaving for Minnesota. Don't be impulsive. You aren't that girl anymore."

"This isn't about you, Ellis."

"What about us? You've come up with this weird conspiracy that your brother's death was so much different than other soldiers who died over there. It's war."

"Mom and Dad thought information was withheld from them, too. It's not just me. Perry's been gone almost three years. It's not impulsive."

"I won't stand by while you run off digging up skeletons."

"Look, I have to go. Are you coming or not?"

Then he'd played the trump card. *"No, I'm not. If you go, you're going to throw us away."*

Wild child Abbi had reared her head, announced they were done, and walked off.

The conversation still upset her, a perfect example of how he had controlled her, and how she'd allowed it. Abbi grabbed her tote bag and went to her car. She wasn't going to head to Cash's right away. A responsible guest would bring a food item to contribute for lunch.

CHAPTER 5

Cash stared at the food lining the counter. He'd grilled burgers. Then doubt had assailed him and he'd wondered if Abbi was fucking vegetarian or something. So he'd grilled kabobs with mushrooms, bell peppers, and onions.

Then he'd wondered if dessert was expected at a lunch date, so he'd grilled pineapple.

Then he'd wondered if Abbi liked grilled food at all.

He was a one-trick pony. He manned a mean grill and defaulted to the oven if the weather was atrocious, as it easily could be in Minnesota.

A knock yanked him out of his food troubles.

"Come in," he called, then winced. He should answer the door. That's what people did when they had someone over for lunch.

But this wasn't a date, so it didn't matter.

Her footsteps echoed through the house. "Cash?"

"In the kitchen." The old farmhouse's kitchen was separate from the rest of the house, but Abbi seemed to find it easily enough.

He froze when she walked in. Knowing she was coming over the last twelve hours should've prepared him, but here she was, in his house. His guilt reared up that he was just stringing her along, his longing to touch her soft skin almost overrode his manners, and the conflicting feelings of wanting her to leave town and fearing she'd do just that…it all robbed him of words.

Or it might've been her appearance. She was tempting in her athletic clothes with her hair pulled back. He'd nibbled that neck before.

Did she remember?

From the flush staining her cheeks, she just might.

He lamely waved his tongs over the plates of food. "I didn't know what you'd like. I just grilled burgers."

Her mouth parted while she looked over the food. She held up a bag he hadn't noticed. "That's perfect. I brought some chips. Hope you like Cool Ranch…" She wandered over to the tray of fruit. "Is that grilled pineapple?"

"Yeah, they were on sale." Pineapples were a safe topic. Could they stick to that all afternoon?

"I love pineapple, but I've never tried it grilled." She handed him the bag and snagged a ring.

He relaxed as she chewed. They were just hanging out. If she wasn't making a big deal out of this, then he wouldn't, either.

Her eyes drifted closed. "Mmm, this is really good. It brings out the sweetness, but the smokiness gives it a whole new flair."

Her lips glistened with pineapple. If he kissed her, would he taste the same thing she did?

Her eyes flew open. "Oh, I'm sorry. How rude, huh?" She searched the counter.

He lifted a plate from behind him and handed it to her. "Don't worry, we're pretty informal around here. We eat standing or sitting, or bring it on the go. Go ahead and fill your plate. It's a little breezy out, so we should eat inside at least."

She shot him a grateful smile and did as he said while he opened the chips and retrieved mineral waters for them. No alcohol today. He wanted her reaction to him to be organic.

They settled at the table. He arranged his silverware around his plate. Then switched it around, then just set it on his plate in frustration. This was just lunch between two people who had to talk. Not two people who spent an amazing night together playing with each other's bodies.

From the way she dug into her burger, she didn't have the same reservations. Of course, she didn't remember like he did. Drunk. She'd been so open and full of laughter, he'd had no idea alcohol had been fueling her night.

With a bitter taste in his mouth, he dug into his food and froze again when Abbi groaned.

"I was so hungry," she said around her mouthful. She swallowed and continued. "I went for a run this morning and haven't eaten since. Probably not the best idea."

"We never have to worry about refueling with protein here. We always have fresh eggs and freezers full of meat."

"Sounds delicious." Another groan escaped. "I miss red meat."

He choked on a chip, and a blush stained her cheeks.

"I mean, if I never see another chicken breast, it will be too soon."

"But has your chicken been brined and grilled, because that, honey, you can never have too much of."

"Seasoned, plain or in a salad, it's all been done way too much." She set down her burger, took the top off, and loaded it up with grilled veggies.

The corner of Cash's mouth twitched. His cousins often did the same thing.

"You like to grill?" she asked.

"No."

She stopped and he laughed.

"If it wasn't for the grill," he amended, "I'd probably starve. I'm not an oven guy."

This was the Abbi he remembered. Easy conversation, easy laughter. Something he didn't often experience outside of family. At his age, women were looking for a night of fun that'd lead to a long-term relationship and since he had a reputation, they put extra effort into trying to tame Cash Walker. He often fantasized about a real relationship, but then his parents would visit. And there was the reminder.

"Where are you staying now?" he asked as he finished his meal.

She polished off her last bite. "I'm at the Nightstays. It's a little more expensive, but the room's bigger and since I was staying so long, I wanted the comfort." A smile curved her lush lips. "It doesn't smell like an old dishrag and the owner hasn't tried setting me up with anyone."

"Because those owners have children still in elementary school. Give 'em time."

She giggled and they fell quiet for a moment.

Cash cleared his throat. He knew he couldn't avoid the real reason why she was here forever, but he'd try. "Are you… just here for a few days?"

"I had two weeks of vacation. El—I had nothing else planned, so I used it to come here. I don't know how long I'll be here."

"What do you do for a living?"

Her tone went flat. "I'm a bank teller."

"That bad?" He'd never given the occupation a second thought. His bank was his parents' bank, and his grandparents' bank. He'd known all the employees for ages, even gone to school with some.

"No, it's just not my thing."

"Then why work there?" He couldn't imagine not waking up and ranching every day. He'd lived that nightmare for eight long years, but it'd been better than being at home at the time. When Dillon had gotten out of the army, Cash couldn't stand to be in the military without his cousin and had gotten out, too. Thankfully, when he'd moved back home, his aunts and uncles had sold the Walker Five operation to Cash and his four cousins—and his parents had moved away.

"It's a respectable job. It pays the bills." It had the ring of a pep talk she gave herself before each shift.

"There's lots of those that do both and you can enjoy. What'd you go to school for?"

Her gaze darted away and she shifted in her chair. "Visual arts."

Cash reclined in his seat and folded his arms. "Yeah, I can see how it can be hard to find work in that field in a small town, but there's gotta be something."

She gave him a look he couldn't interpret. "I'm sure there is. So…"

Aw, shit. Here it was.

"You and my brother were good friends?"

Cash regretted his last handful of chips as they formed a lump in his gut. "He joined the unit a couple of years before he… Yeah, we were friends."

"How often were you deployed?"

Cash readjusted his hat. He should've taken it off for lunch, but he wasn't used to special occasions. "Three times. The first two weren't uneventful, but nothing occurred like what happened to your brother."

"How soon afterward did you get out of the army?"

This was starting to feel like an interview. He expected her to pull out a notebook and pencil from the bag she'd left on the kitchen counter.

"As soon as that deployment was over." He'd been signing papers as soon as his boots had hit the ground.

"Did you ever think of visiting my parents?"

Good lord, no. And say what? His throat grew thick with panic. Facing Daniels's parents? While he'd come home alive? No. Nope. He wasn't going to reopen the worst wound they'd ever received.

His phone saved him. "Excuse me." He shot up to answer it and left the room.

His cousin Brock got right to the point. "Dude, can you take over for me?"

"Yeah." Cash didn't care why Brock asked, it was a way out of Abbi's interrogation.

"Can you do it now? Josie just got notice that her brother's getting transferred to the prison in St. Cloud."

Cash tamped down the irritation that stirred when Brock discussed his new girlfriend. It was his issue, not Brock's. He had a hard time letting go of his protective nature, ever since he'd first seen Brock getting laughed at on the playground. It was harder now that Brock had admitted he was autistic. But they were both adults, and Brock was in love. Cash was still accepting that it wasn't his business.

"Are you in the east section today?" Cash mentally prepared his speech to tell Abbi why he had to jet.

"Yes, I'll leave the combine parked at the approach. Aaron's running the truck to empty the hoppers. I'll catch a ride from him."

"Got it." Cash hung up and found Abbi picking at an almost empty plate of pineapple.

"You know what would make this really good?" she asked as he entered the dining room. "Whipped cream. Especially if the pineapple was still hot off the grill."

If she'd make that noise again over how delicious it was,

he would buy five cans of whipped cream and two more pineapples this afternoon. He shook his desire off. He'd already tapped that, and she was going to be pissed at him when he left anyway.

"Sorry to cut this short. I've gotta get to work earlier than I thought."

Abbi pursed her lips and narrowed her eyes on him. Was he transparent? "And when can we talk?" Her words were frosty.

He checked the weather app on his phone. "Rain's forecasted by Wednesday. If it rains, we can take a breather harvesting."

"Wednesday? It's only Sunday." She slapped her hands on her legs and stood. "Is harvest the reason why you can't make time?"

He nodded. As an excuse, there were worse ones.

"Then why I don't I come with?"

His eyes widened. "Where? In the *combine?*"

She smiled like she'd busted him in a lie. "Why not? My grandpa farmed, and I remember combines can seat more than one. I can follow you and hop in, and hop back out when we're done talking."

She made it sound so easy. It sounded more like a nightmare to him.

"You can't tell me you've never had a girl in the combine with you," she teased.

Shock and the urge to run made it hard to comprehend her question. "No," he managed to get out. "No, I haven't."

He backed up as she rose. She fully intended to come with him. Why was he feeling like he was anticipating another date? Why did spending the afternoon with her in tightly enclosed quarters sound so…not awful?

She wanted to discuss her brother. He could respect that, but he couldn't rehash that experience. It'd almost destroyed

Dillon, and he didn't want his own thoughts and speculations to harm Abbi in any way. Right now, she had everyone else to blame about her brother's death. Her parents probably held themselves accountable to some extent. It was natural. But they could blame the army, they could blame the war, hell, they could blame Cash and Dillon and the other guys in their platoon. If he admitted that "hey, I think your boy got himself blown up on purpose so you could have his life insurance money," what would it do to them?

Abbi's tenacity at ferreting out the complete story would only lead to heartbreak.

His mind spun, trying to figure out how to say no. He strongly suspected she'd chase him out to the field.

Suddenly, an idea blossomed.

A slow grin spread across Cash's chiseled face.

He was up to something. She'd suspected the harvest excuse was just to get out of talking about Perry. Cash had looked like he was ready to keel over at the idea of her accompanying him to work. But now…

"Well, now, I'm sure you'd love to ride in the combine, but it can be a long and boring afternoon. If you really want to come with, you can drive truck."

"What truck? Your pickup?" Would riding in his pickup jog more memories of their night together? She was getting snippets, but not fine details. The memories were full of naked skin and pleasure, but she couldn't recall exactly how he'd tasted, how hot his kisses had been. She remembered laughing and enjoying herself, but what had they talked about?

"The grain truck."

Oh, to drive alongside the combine to be filled. Her dad

used to talk about driving the grain truck to haul the harvest to the silos. "Don't I need a special license?"

He frowned. "I don't know. You gonna crash it?"

"I might if you keep refusing to talk to me."

A heavy sigh escaped him. "I don't have anything to talk with you about, Abbi. I don't know what you're looking for."

She tilted her head and considered him. His tone was so serious, so…withdrawn. No, she believed there was something he didn't want to discuss. Was it selfish of her to think it was something he *needed* to talk about?

Maybe if she appeased his panic, he'd open up. "I understand that it's not a subject you're jumping up and down about. I get it. But I took vacation and I'm here. Can I come with you and you can at least share some stories about him?"

This deer in the headlights looked even more ready to bolt. The deer analogy made her think of his horse.

"How's Patsy Cline?"

"Recovering." For the first time since she asked about going with him, he seemed to inhale fully. "She struggles with bouts of colic. Her old owner sold her for dirt cheap 'cause he was tired of dealin' with it. She's the best purchase I've ever made."

Abbi smiled at his dedication to a creature no one wanted. "Good."

He gave all he had to his horse. Did he offer the same to his women?

She was stricken with indecision. How long was she going to chase after Cash and nag him about Perry? Maybe she should come back another time.

Her hopes fell further.

Should she go home? Should she even bother talking with Dillon Walker? It was one thing to have the nerve to drive up to a strange man's place, asking about her brother. But would she have been as persistent with Cash if she hadn't jumped into bed with him first?

Would Dillon be as hospitable to a stranger, or would he run her off?

Maybe she could just ask. "Does Dillon know I've come by?"

Cash's features returned to serious. "Yes, I've talked with him."

"Oh, okay." She was learning what crestfallen felt like. How dismal returning to Green Bay and her job was becoming. She'd have to move out of Ellis's place—if he hadn't already organized, labeled, and packed her stuff.

The room closed in on her. What was she doing here? It was a lost cause. A fool's errand because she missed her brother. Ellis was right. It had been impulsive. She'd been impulsive and she was intruding on a family and their work.

"I'll gather my things. I'm really sorry, Cash. I shouldn't have bothered you. I can see..." She was going to start bawling if she kept explaining herself. She darted to the kitchen instead to gather her tote, which held her car keys and wallet. Cash could keep the rest. He'd been more than generous.

He was right behind her; she jumped when he spoke.

"Where are you going to go?"

Home was on the tip of her tongue, but no. "The Twin Cities aren't far away. They have a free zoo. Maybe I could go to the Mall of America." And shop with what money?

"Sounds nice." Cash shoved his hands in his pockets, took one out and adjusted his hat, shoved it back in his pocket.

She draped the bag's straps over her shoulder, but he was standing between her and the kitchen door. If he didn't move, she'd plow him over to leave before the tears fell.

"Look, you're already here," he said. "Why don't you just ride out with me to take over the combine."

A surge of hope rose, but she feared he'd take it back if she agreed. She clenched the straps of her bag. "I'm not relegated to grain truck duty?"

"I know this is hard for both of us," he continued. "I understand where you're coming from, I really do. So why don't we just hang out and swap Daniels—Perry—stories."

She snatched up the olive branch. "What do I need to pack?"

CHAPTER 6

*A*bbi had expected meeting one of Cash's cousins to be awkward. The driver of the combine was gone, but Aaron had been waiting for them in the grain truck; Cash hadn't needed someone for it. When Aaron spotted them, he'd hopped out of the vehicle and rushed over, almost wiping out in the field in his haste.

Aaron had reddish-blond hair and startling blue eyes like Cash. Not as brilliant, crystal blue, but stunning on their own.

She wondered how Cash would introduce her, but he did it smoothly. "She's the sister of an army buddy we lost in Iraq."

Aaron's eyes flared, but he recovered his composure quickly and shook her hand. "I'm sorry for your loss. Have you talked to Dillon yet?"

She opened her mouth to answer, but Cash beat her to it. "No. I'll give him a call and see if he can meet us later."

Abbi restrained herself from throwing a hug around Cash's broad shoulders. He'd almost shut her down cold yesterday, and again today, but now he was going out of his way to help her.

Cash and Aaron discussed plans for finishing this field. Abbi soaked in the farmer speak. Her grandpa had died when she was a teenager, but she'd gotten to spend several summers running through corn rows and crawling over hay bales.

Aaron jogged back to the white grain truck, but not before he cast a speculative look toward her and Cash. Yeah, she knew how it looked. A man like Cash didn't bring a girl around out of pure friendship, maybe not ever, so her standing here was a big deal.

Crowding into the combine with Cash was almost as intimate as being in the same bed. They were fully clothed this time, and floor-to-ceiling windows surrounded them, but it was just them, side by side.

Cash fiddled with the radio but kept the volume down. He flipped on the computer and punched in some buttons. Abbi craned her neck to take it all in. The control console was way more complex than a video game. Switches and levers lined one side, there had to be about twenty of them. A screen was positioned over them and another controller looked like a joystick.

Cash noticed her inspection. "It's called precision farming. Probably not what your granddaddy did."

"Oh, he was precise." She chuckled. "Most Midwest farmers don't let anything go to waste."

"Yes, we always tried to optimize our yield, but now we have GPS guiding the tractor so not one stalk of corn or one soybean plant goes to waste."

"What happened to wheat?" Golden fields were everywhere, but she hadn't seen much for wheat on the Walker's land.

"We still grow wheat and sunflowers, the standards.

Beans are the shit now. Canola. I wish we lived closer to a sugar beet processing plant. Sugar beets can make it a good year if gas prices are down; otherwise hauling them is costly. We get together and plan each year depending on the markets."

The ride wasn't as bumpy as expected and Abbi relaxed into her seat while Cash drove. The grain sprayed right into the truck and when it was full, he shut the auger off. The hopper was almost full by the time Aaron got back from emptying his load into the grain bins. Cash and Aaron worked together seamlessly; this was obviously a process they'd been doing as soon as they could drive—probably before they'd gotten their licenses.

He lumbered to a stop. "The hopper's full. Aaron'll be back soon. We try to have more than one driver, but sometimes the fields argue with us and want to be harvested on top of each other. Dillon and Travis are working on another section and Brock'll jump in with another truck when he gets back."

"Grandpa used to work with his neighbors. There'd be like three or four combines working a stretch." She smiled and angled toward him. "I always thought it was neat when it got dark and you could see these massive machines out there, with lights that rivaled football stadiums."

Cash grinned in return. "You should've caught us a month ago. That's exactly what it was like." He pointed off in the distance. She stretched until she could make out a copse of trees and silver bins poking over the top. "That's the neighbor we team up with most years. Another neighbor is closer, but when he died, the farm died with him. Not that he would've helped us anyway."

She caught his gaze and they both froze. They were inches apart and his scent surrounded her. He smelled wild, like the great outdoors—and she liked wild.

Her gaze dipped down to his lips. This close, tastes and textures flooded her brain. She'd nibbled on him that night, and she wanted to do it again, only one hundred percent sober.

He swayed closer; she inched toward him.

The sharp bleat of a horn startled both of them.

Cash swore and twisted to look out the window. Aaron had arrived and given the warning honk for Cash to start moving.

They lurched forward. Abbi's pounding heart faded in disappointment. A kiss from Cash would've been worth the epically bad decision.

"These are the straggler crops." Cash's tone was light, like they'd never been about to make out. "We pick them off as they're ready. Does your grandpa still farm?"

"No, he and Grandma passed away already."

"I have a gram still in the nursing home. She's a firecracker, but her body can't keep up with all her crazy ideas. Gramps died ten or so years ago. I live in their old house."

"That house is so cute, so much character." And that enviable front porch. The stifling apartment Ellis had secured for them didn't even have a small deck.

"I was raised in it. Gramps sold the farm and ranch to his five boys. My dad got their old house and they moved to town but didn't exactly retire. Gramps worked out here every day until he died. I wish I could care for it like it needed, but—" he gave her a sheepish smile, "—I'd rather be outside working."

"You must have a lot of outdoor work with the cattle, the horses, and the farm."

"It's great." God, his smile should be outlawed. "I ride horse whenever possible. I enjoy this, too." He swept his arm around the interior of the combine. "As long as I don't have to do it day in and day out. The other guys enjoy it more, except for Brock. He'd rather be digging in an engine."

She sighed wistfully. "I sit inside all day. Some days are so busy, not even the clock moves forward and it feels like forever."

Ellis kept telling her she'd get used to it, but each year she was a little unhappier.

Cash's work sounded adult and responsible, but he loved it. She wanted a job she could love, or at least one that wouldn't suck the life out of her. She wasn't meant to nine-to-five it, with the occasional Saturday morning. She wanted to *live*. "Ride a horse every day… I've never ridden."

Cash whipped his head toward her. "Never? Oh, honey, we'll have to change that."

She giggled and ignored the melancholy tug on her heart. He probably called all the girls "honey." She shouldn't like it so much.

"What are you doing tomorrow?" A casual question. He was watching the rows and the path of the lumbering beast intently, but she sensed a deeper thread of…something…to it. Was he asking her out? They still hadn't discussed her brother, yet he wasn't getting rid of her.

"Uh, I'm doing nothing tomorrow," she said with a laugh. She had over a week and a half left of nothing.

"Then we'll cure that never-ridden-a-horse affliction you have."

She sucked in a delighted breath and gripped his shoulder. "Are you serious? Is your horse okay to ride?"

"She's as good as new." His bemused expression was almost a full smile, but he didn't shake her off. "I have something to do in the morning, but I'll be home before lunch. And I have a ton of leftovers to eat. Except for the pineapple. That's all gone for some reason," he drawled.

She playfully swatted him and kept her hands off him after that. Touching him was like a primal need.

"I'll pick up another one, though," he offered, "with some whipped cream."

She moaned. "Yes! What else can we grill?"

He chuckled. "Anything and everything. Unless it's twenty below or thirty-mile-an-hour winds, I cook with the grill."

Her nonexistent deck made grilling frustrating.

"Peaches are good, but we might've missed the season. Wanna try bananas?"

"With whipped cream?"

"Yes, ma'am."

She clapped her hands with glee. This is what she'd been missing since Perry died—fun. Her smile faded. She missed joking around with him, with someone who understood her.

Cash's hand landed on her knee with a reassuring rub. "What's going on? You grew quiet."

Tears threatened to well and she swallowed hard. "Losing my brother just hits me sometimes. Especially if it brings up buried memories." Suddenly, she couldn't stop talking even if she'd staple her mouth shut. "Like, when I laugh. God, I hadn't realized how much I don't just joke around anymore. When did all the fun go away? When did I become so boring that I never laugh anymore? Perry used to needle me constantly, always with the hard time, and I loved and hated him for it, but now that he's gone, I love him so much for giving me those times."

She sniffled, fighting to remain composed.

He stroked her thigh and found her hand to give it a squeeze. "Honestly, he hasn't been gone that long. Sometimes, it feels like yesterday, that'll I wake up and be sleeping in a tent with nine other guys." He shuddered and his mouth turned down. Perry had had the same reaction about being in the military. She'd often asked him why he stayed in. *What else am I good for, Abs?* Anything and everything, she'd shot back. She was the one who limped through college and would rather slam a six-pack than stay up late studying.

Cash's thumb stroked her hand. "But when I'm out in the pastures fixing fence, those eight years feel like they never happened. Like I never left Moore. It's weird."

"Do you miss any of it?" She inched as close to him as the seat would allow. The interior of the cab was comfortable, luxurious almost, but the topic left her chilled.

He lifted a shoulder and his gaze drifted around, monitoring the combine's progress. "Very little. I got to see some of the world, have some new experiences. I think it made me more disciplined with my ranching. I'm up at dawn and outside working. I put in long days, but it's still on my schedule, even though the animals and the weather dictate what I do with my time."

"Yeah, I can see that." Maybe Perry had craved the discipline. He'd been a guy who flitted from interest to interest, almost dispirited at times, but never when he talked with her. "Do you have siblings?"

"A sister. She's almost eight years younger than me. In her second year of college."

The flat tone of his made her wince. Was that how Perry had sounded about her in school? "She worries you?"

"She's aimless." He shook his head. "If I could buy her self-esteem, I would. For the life of me, I can't understand why she lets the guys in her life treat her like shit. No, I understand why and—" He clamped his mouth shut.

She waited, but he didn't elaborate. "I think Perry worried about the same thing, if it makes you feel any better."

He frowned at her, his eyes filled with a stormy emotion she couldn't identify. It drained away to be replaced with his typical good humor. "Hey, we're almost done."

Jovial Cash was the man he showed to the world. He was a person with deep emotions, but when he interacted with people, he was always Happy Cash.

Their conversation switched to a rundown of what they'd do when they wrapped up this field. She drove Cash's pickup, which was like steering a ship compared to her Acura, and followed the combine and grain truck back to Aaron's place.

The expanse of their operation was impressive. Had to be to support five employees. Cash mentioned he was one of the oldest of the cousins he ran the business with. They must all be close to getting married and starting families, which was even more incentive to keep the business strong.

She grew envious. A family with strong support. Did any of the Walkers have to change themselves to appease their relatives?

Enough of the pity party. She focused on driving her first ever Ford F250, with the seat moved a good foot forward. She didn't have Cash's long legs.

After all the equipment was stored for the night, Cash hopped in. She drove them back to his place.

He sat forward when she turned into his drive.

A maroon hybrid SUV sat in front of the house next to Abbi's car.

Cash waved to his parking spot in front of the detached garage. "Just park there. Mom's blocking my garage stall."

Abbi squeezed the wheel. His mother. Abbi had planned to drift into Moore, find Reno Walker, talk, and mosey back out. But she was meeting more and more of the family. It was harder and harder to remember her original purpose in Moore.

~

Cash saw his mom's vehicle and was tempted to direct Abbi to head to the highway and just drive, anywhere.

Despite the feels in the combine when they'd hit the topic of their siblings, he'd had an enjoyable afternoon. And introducing someone to the bliss of riding horse was always a privilege. He looked forward to the next day, both getting to jump back on Patsy Cline but also seeing how Abbi would take to Mandrell.

But his mom's SUV was like an ominous dark cloud heralding a shit-filled night. Mom never drove down on her own unless it was to cry about Dad. Maybe she didn't realize how much responsibility Cash took for her troubles with his dad. Maybe she did, and it was Cash's price to pay for being born.

Having his mom in town when he went on his Monday-morning errand only fed the well of guilt. Arranging a horse outing after his Monday-morning breakfast at the Brown House Cafe had been partly selfish, something to look forward to after feeling like he'd betrayed his mom.

He got out of the pickup and walked Abbi to her car.

"I left my stuff in the house. I at least need my keys."

Yep. Because that's how his luck was going the last two days. "I'll go get it. Wait here."

She gave him a funny look but thankfully didn't argue. She must think he didn't want to introduce her to his mother. He didn't, but not for the reason she might assume. His mom's assumptions might get the best of him, and he didn't need another lecture on how being responsible for a woman's heart was for an honorable man and he needed to ensure he was up to the task before entering into something as serious as a relationship.

He slogged to the house, his Tony Martins as heavy as feed-sacks.

Mom sat at the table with her head buried in her hands.

For a fleeting moment, he hoped he could grab Abbi's items from the kitchen and get out before his mom noticed. But she had to have heard him pull up.

The door hinges squeaked and his boots on the hardwood couldn't pull off stealth.

Mom's head popped up. Her eyes were red rimmed and her nose was puffy.

What had Dad done now? He didn't stop but aimed for the kitchen. "I just gotta grab something and bring it outside. I'll be right back."

"We're getting divorced."

Hit boots hit with a thud as he stopped and closed his eyes. Divorced? After all Mom had stuck through? Why now? She had held on for almost thirty years. Dad's screw-up must've been epic.

He opened his eyes and adopted the emotional numbness he usually did when around his parents. "Who asked for the divorce?"

"I did." She blew her nose and added the tissue to the growing pile in front of her. Her brown hair was neatly combed and she wore her standard jeans and conservative top. Mom would call her looks average, but then, undercutting herself was like a hobby. And when people commented on how they didn't look alike, it broke his heart as much as hers. Yes, he had his dad's blue eyes and build, but the rest was a reminder of Dad's betrayal.

"I couldn't take the last one," she said, her voice breaking. "He refused to quit seeing her."

Cash just nodded. Same old story, only Mom had finally drawn the line. And Dad had stepped over it, like he always did.

"I…have a new place. I just wanted to tell you in person."

"Does Sissy know?"

"Hannah hates it when you call her that, you know."

Another item he did wrong according to his mother. "No, not yet. I'd like to stay over and drive there tomorrow. St. Cloud is too far for today, but I want her to hear before the wildfire gossip spreads. I'm sure Allan will tell his whore and who knows who she'll spill it to."

He didn't flinch at her naming-calling. He couldn't blame her and it was nothing new. "Is she from Moore?" His parents had moved far from Moore to Eden Prairie. Instead of getting away from all the drama, it had opened a new playing field for his dad.

"No, but it's a small world."

No, Mom had wanted to tell Cash in person. Cash could take the news. Sissy would collapse in tears like she always did when Mom and Dad fought.

"I deserve better," his mom said adamantly.

"I know you do," was Cash's automatic response.

A soft squeak of floorboard made them both swing around. Mom's mouth fell open.

Abbi's eyes were wide. She took a step back as if she were going to run out the way she'd come. "I'm so sorry. I just need to grab my stuff."

She looked so apologetic he had to say something. "No problem, Abbi."

Abbi scurried into the kitchen and right back out with her tote. She breezed past Cash. "Call you tomorrow," she said quietly as she passed.

She'd interpreted the gravity of the situation and didn't linger. At least he had that going for him. Awkwardness on top of all this angst might break his mom.

"Who was that?" Mom asked. Her eyes watered again.

He gave her his standard spiel of an army buddy's sister.

"Oh, Cash. Of all people, why get involved with Perry Daniels's sister? Isn't there another woman who hasn't gone through what she has?" The disappointment in her voice usually washed off him, but not today.

"I'm not Dad," he said tightly. He should say they weren't involved and get his mom off the topic, but her lectures weren't welcome today.

Her mouth flattened. "I didn't say you were. But a girl who's going through what she did doesn't need a man who plays with her emotions."

She walked out on me, he wanted to say, but that'd reveal he and Abbi had already had relations. And when had he ever played with a girl's emotions? Thanks to Mom, that was one thing he did really well. "We're just talking. She wants to talk about her brother; I'm not going to send her packing."

He didn't mention he'd already tried. No one could send Abbi away if she didn't want to go. He nearly smiled at the thought but didn't out of respect for his mom.

He got the Mom stare for another second before she finally stood and gathered her pile of tissues. "Go do your chores. I'll make some dinner."

He rubbed his eyes as he walked out of the house. Tomorrow morning, he'd have to sneak away without his mom knowing where he went. He'd gotten to a point where Monday mornings felt less like a duty and more like something to look forward to. After today, he'd need someone to talk to who knew his situation. But the horse ride with Abbi was enough to get him through the rest of the night with his mother and her tears.

CHAPTER 7

$\mathcal{C}$ash arrived at the Brown House Cafe shortly after nine in the morning. This was the best time. He missed the breakfast rush and Frankie could take her coffee break with him after having opened the diner and worked her ass off all morning.

He picked one of his three usual booths. Always in Frankie's section. He couldn't find her, but maybe she was bustling around in the kitchen. Frankie didn't quit moving even if he urged her to quit working herself into the ground.

"Cash?"

Abbi's voice was a balm, overriding the flush of panic that he'd have to explain why he was here. "Morning, Abbi."

She slid in across from him. Her hair hung damp and she was in the jeans and sweater he'd recommended for riding. She must've done laundry at the hotel; she was wearing the sweater she'd gotten sick in. Still cute in it, too.

"I'm not stalking you, I promise. The girl working the front desk of the hotel swore this was the best place to get an omelet."

"She wasn't lying." Cash smiled politely as he searched for

Frankie. His smile vanished as one of the other servers bustled toward him.

"Cash, are you here for Frankie?" Carol, a good friend of Frankie's, stood barely above five feet tall with hair long gone gray.

The way Carol asked him spiked his worry, but the way she ignored the woman across from him was downright troubling. He'd never brought someone with him in all the Mondays he'd met with Frankie. "What's wrong?"

Carol laid a hand on his shoulder. "She was admitted to the hospital last night."

Cash was already scooting out of the booth. Abbi was doing the same.

"What happened?" he asked.

"We're not sure, yet, but you let her know we're thinking about her."

He pulled Carol in for a half hug. "Thanks for letting me know."

She patted him on the back. "Tell her I'm stopping by and forcing my help on her whether she likes it or not."

"Will do."

Abbi was on his heels as he left the cafe. "Who's Frankie? And how's your mom?"

Cash should've realized that after last night, this morning would roll downhill quicker than shit in a rainstorm. He'd answered Abbi's questions only because she appeared genuinely concerned, and dammit, his family drama was piling so high that it was nice to have someone to talk to. "Frankie's like a grandmother to me." Not a lie. "My mom and dad are getting divorced, so what you saw yesterday is pretty much how she's doing."

Abbi went around to the passenger side of his pickup and he didn't hesitate to let her in.

"Aren't you going to miss breakfast?" he asked as he backed out of his parking spot.

"Yes, but the cafe will be here tomorrow. And the next day. You looked a little haggard when I arrived, but after you heard about the hospital…" She shrugged. "I didn't want to leave you alone."

He looked like he felt and he didn't care. If Abbi was coming with him—and he wanted her with him—he didn't want to censor himself. He found himself spilling the history that he never talked about and that no one ever brought up. Not even his mom—she just constantly alluded to it.

"Frankie is more than *like* my grandma."

Abbi's forehead wrinkled in confusion.

"My mom that you sort of met yesterday isn't my birth mom." He blew out a gusty breath and explained. "My dad cheated on her with Frankie's daughter shortly after they were married. My birth mom didn't want me, already had some other guy and wanted to move away, so she called Dad from the hospital and told him to pick me up or she was signing me over to the adoption agency. Frankie's my grandma."

"Holy shit!" Abbi grabbed his hand and squeezed it. Her gesture reminded him of when he'd done the same thing in the combine when she'd been upset thinking about her brother.

Had he ever spoken his personal details out loud?

No, he hadn't. It wasn't necessary when living in a small town where everyone knew his business. Most days, he could pretend no one knew, or that no one cared, but they did. Whether it was whispers from the older ladies at church, or the knowing glances from Frankie's crew at her work, his origins made great fodder for gossip.

His cousins never mentioned it. To them, his mom was Aunt Patty, their aunt, and he was their cousin. His mom never mentioned it, either—directly. She was his mom. Period. He was her son. Period. But it didn't mean his mom wouldn't hold his dad's and birth mom's behavior over him.

He knew Mom hadn't meant to. She'd wanted to raise him right. Raise a gentleman, a man worthy of a woman's love. The intended effect hadn't happened. Instead, he avoided relationships to avoid becoming the man she feared.

Abbi was watching him. He reluctantly withdrew his hand to navigate the roads.

"Mom forgave Dad, at least that time, and raised me like her own."

"At least that time? Do you have more half siblings?"

Discussing his family's worst-kept secret left a sour taste in his mouth. It was freeing to openly talk about it—to a point. It was still about his dad, a man he looked up to, promiscuous ways aside. "Just my sister, Hannah, but she's not from another woman. As far as I know, my dad often seeks company in someone else's bed, but he hasn't repeated the same mistake he made with me."

He fisted his hands around the wheel.

"I'm sorry."

"He's a good guy, but his strengths aren't in being faithful to his wife."

"Where's your birth mom?"

"Dead, and before you say sorry, I never met her. Not that it isn't terrible," he added quickly. "I just never knew her and she never wanted me. But her death almost killed Frankie."

That was the real tragedy about his birth mom's death. He couldn't summon anything beyond ambivalence, but he had a huge family and a lot of support. Frankie was alone.

"What happened?" Abbi's presence washed over him. His anxiety over Frankie would've chewed him up on the way to the hospital, and even though the subject was an ever-healing wound, having Abbi here made it bearable. He was terribly glad she'd come with him.

"Suicide. The guy she left with was an over-controlling bastard. Frankie ran herself dry trying to help my—Holly—get away, but she must've felt trapped. I guess I was only five when she killed herself."

Abbi probably noticed his quick switch, but he tried not to refer to Holly as his mom. She'd birthed him, but Mom was his mom.

"I'm still really sorry. Have you and Frankie been close your whole life?"

He wished, and he had serious regrets that they hadn't been. "Actually, no. She found me when I was eighteen and told me about Holly. Thought I should know because Mom and Dad told her they refused to talk to me about her, which meant they didn't want Frankie around, either. She waited until I was old enough to decide for myself. After that, I started stopping in at the cafe now and again. My parents, of course, avoid the place."

"That's so sad. You didn't know you had another grandma in town?"

He maneuvered into the hospital parking lot. "No. I never gave Holly much thought. By the time they told me Mom had adopted me, it mattered, but it didn't."

Maybe he'd buy that line himself one day. It'd fucked him up. And then he'd gotten over it. Mostly. Until he was eighteen and Frankie had caught him gassing up his pickup one night before finding a bonfire and some girls to party with.

Forget the girls. That night, he'd drunk whatever he could get his hands on and gotten shit-faced. Not long after that, Dillon had spouted off about enlisting and there was Cash's ass next to him, raising his right hand and swearing an oath of enlistment for the army.

He and Abbi rushed into the hospital and inquired about

the room number at the front desk. Abbi had claimed his hand somewhere en route.

"Frankie?" the matronly receptionist asked.

"Frances Samuelson," Cash answered, grateful he knew that much about his own grandmother.

"Room 205." She leaned over the desk and pointed down the hall. "Catch the elevator at the end of the hall, and once you get off, the room will be on your left."

He thanked her and took off, towing Abbi behind him.

Abbi clutched Cash's hand. Distress pinched the corners of his eyes as they rode the elevator up.

The story of his life was *tragic*. Her parents were a pain in her ass, but her dad had showered her mom with romantic gestures. Did he still? Abbi would have to remind him, make sure he was keeping the love alive after Perry's death.

When they stepped onto the second floor, warmth surrounded her. It felt good after being outside in the chill with just a sweatshirt, but if she had to work here all day, she'd suffer heat exhaustion. The temperature hike must be for the patients' benefit.

They located room 205 and Cash peeked inside. She waited to follow his lead. She'd expected a grandmotherly woman, but a lady with graying blond hair rested on the bed. She was probably a little shorter than her and slender, like she'd run her ass off at her serving job her whole life. Lines of stress and worry marred her ruddy skin. The sound of a blood-pressure machine filled the room. Abbi followed the cord on the cuff around Frankie's arm to a large standalone machine. The screen of the machine was littered with numbers.

Frankie's pale brows rose in surprise. "Cash, what a

surprise." Her gaze touched on Abbi and her eyes brightened. Frankie shifted in an attempt to cover herself, but two cords draped out of the neck of her hospital gown.

"Hey, Frankie. I hope you don't mind that I brought a friend, although I don't think I could've stopped her." Cash gave Frankie his award-winning smile. "This is Abbi Daniels."

Oh my... His dazzling smile was totally a cover. Abbi remembered it from the night they'd met. It's what had made her practically beg him to drive her back to her room. Had it been genuine, or a way to fool the ladies that he was only good for one night?

She might have intruded, but she didn't regret it. Getting to know him was worth it. "I happened to be at the cafe when Cash heard you were in here. I kind of gave him no choice but to bring me."

"That's fine." Frankie pushed a button to raise the head of her bed. "I'm afraid they're overreacting anyway."

"Really?"

At Cash's disbelieving tone, Frankie flushed. "It was just a dizzy spell."

"Did you topple over this morning before you started your shift?" Cash disengaged his hand and sat down in one of the two chairs by Frankie's bed. "What's going on, Frankie?"

Frankie tugged gently on the cords attached to her. "They're looking at my heart. Took a gallon of blood in the ER, and a doctor who looks like he should be in preschool admitted me. I'm sure it's nothing."

"Uh-huh. They gotta be thorough."

A middle-aged nurse breezed in and stopped when she spied them. "Oh, hey Cash. Um...I need to check Frankie's vitals, if you don't mind stepping out."

Frankie waved the request off. "It's fine. Not like there's any such thing as privacy in this place."

The nurse smiled. "We make sure you get your money's worth."

She tucked her stethoscope in her ears and listened to Frankie's heart and breathing. While she typed her stats into the computer, she glanced at Cash. "How's it going? I hear your mom's in town. I think she's going to stop by."

Cash stiffened but recovered. If Abbi weren't sitting so close, she might not have noticed. Cash said, "I think she misses working with you guys."

"Well, we miss her. I hope I catch her when she's here." The nurse finished the exam and ambled out.

Frankie studied Cash with her brows drawn together. "Is it okay that you're here?"

Abbi expected the toothpaste-commercial grin, but his small smile was more of an attempt at reassurance.

"I'm an adult and you're my grandmother. Speaking of, what do you need done while you're in here?"

Frankie brushed him off like she had the nurse. "You don't need to worry yourself about me."

"I'm not worried," he replied smoothly, "but your cats might be."

That got Frankie's attention. Her hand flew to her temples. "Oh no. Dutchie is going to be beside herself when I don't come home. Baron might pretend not to care, but he'll make me pay for being gone."

"Gimme your key and we'll stop by and feed them."

Satisfaction rippled through Abbi at his use of "we." Until her phone vibrated. She glanced at the screen. Damn, Ellis and his shit timing.

He'd tried calling the previous night and all morning and she'd ignored him. Texting was his new attempt, but she wasn't going to read it in front of Cash.

Cash lifted a brow as if to ask if everything was all right. She shot him a little smile.

"You sure you don't mind?" Frankie motioned for her purse on the cart next to the bed. Cash handed it off and she dug out a key. "This one's my spare. Why don't you keep it, in case I ever lose my own key or my entire purse. You know where I live, right?"

"Of course." His grandmother shouldn't have to ask him that, but their relationship hadn't been typical.

They stood and he bent to give her a hug. From the shocked but pleased look on Frankie's face, it wasn't a common occurrence. Frankie's hospital episode must've bothered him more than Abbi had realized.

Cash searched out Abbi's hand and they walked out together.

"Aw, shit," he breathed.

Abbi followed his gaze. At the nurse's station, his mom was laughing with three other nurses and aides.

Patty glanced down the hall and her eyes brightened with delight that her son was there, then concern that her son was in the hospital.

Abbi tightened her grip around Cash's hand. He needed it now more than ever.

His mom met them at the elevators. "What are you doing here?"

"Frankie's having some health issues and they're checking her out." His grip was solid iron. Her fingers might be turning white.

Patty drew herself to her full height; her face became a mask. "Oh? And she's doing okay?" Her voice could've rivaled a robot's.

"Seems to be. We'll know after some results come back."

Another we. Abbi didn't know the dynamics between Cash and his mother, but she suspected it was incredibly significant that he was here.

Patty eyed them both. "I...I didn't realize you two

knew…"

Abbi wanted to loosen the collar of her sweater at the tension rippling between mother and son.

"I meet with her every Monday. Have been for a couple years, Mom. And we wrote back and forth when I was in the army."

Patty's brows had risen higher with each sentence. "I see."

Abbi resisted shrinking into Cash when Patty's gaze pinned her.

"I'm sorry, Abbi, we didn't get to officially meet. Patty Walker." She stuck her hand out.

Abbi had to release Cash's hand to shake and when she did, he crossed his arms, his wary gaze still on his mom.

So awkward.

"What else do you two have planned today?" Patty's tone gave Abbi flashbacks to getting grilled by her parents when she went on dates, or out with friends—who were usually covers for going on dates.

"Abbi's never ridden a horse. I have to check on Frankie's place and then we'll go saddle up."

"Take it easy." A hidden warning was in Patty's words.

Cash gave his mom a quick kiss. He grabbed Abbi's hand again and pulled her toward the stairwell.

"Sorry about that," he muttered as they trotted down the stairs.

"Why? That wasn't weird at all."

Cash chuckled and shook his head. "So it was my imagination. I can drop you off at the diner and run to check the cats, if you want to meet in an hour."

"Not a chance." She whispered, "I have a major pussy fetish."

Cash sputtered a cough while she giggled. Juvenile cat jokes to diffuse any lingering unease—worked like a charm.

"What a coincidence," he replied, "so do I."

CHAPTER 8

Frankie's apartment was in an unadorned, white four-plex that had no detached garage, just a large flat of cement for a parking lot. Ceramic planters with withered greens bordered each side of the door. Cash let Abbi into the entryway, where they could find the door to Frankie's unit.

A cloud of stale cigarette smoke hung in the wide hallway. Cash half expected to be hit with the odor of cat urine, but the closer they got to Frankie's door, the more floral the air became.

It bothered him that he didn't know what to expect. She was his grandma and yes, he'd only known for the last ten years and he'd been gone for eight of them, but…she was his grandma.

Was he her only grandchild? Holly was her only child and Frankie had been a single mom. Had Holly tossed more children to their daddies and gone on her way?

He'd ask his parents, but he doubted they knew. As open as Frankie was, she would've told him. Maybe his mom would be more open to his relationship with her now that she was getting divorced.

D-i-v-o-r-c-e. How did an adult kid handle his parents' split? He was an adult. Did that mean it shouldn't bother him? Or that it should upset him less? More? No, it had to be pretty traumatic for a kid. Listening to them argue and then watching Mom dissolve into tears was shittier when he was a kid. If they had split, he would've been shattered. And would've felt one hundred percent responsible. Now, he knew it was mostly on Dad.

It was still shitty as an adult, and it hadn't even fully sunk in yet.

"Nice place." Abbi jerked him out of his musings.

Frankie's place was homey. Colorful needlepoint adorned the walls, flowers and uplifting sayings. Her furniture was dated but in good condition. Candles decorated shelves and end tables, giving the place a fresh atmosphere.

Meows greeted them. A sizeable orange tabby prowled toward them.

"Look at him," Abbi cooed and dropped to a crouch. The cat bypassed her to twine around his legs. Abbi laughed. "You do attract the pussy. Where's the other one?"

"This must be Dutchie, if Baron is the one that acts like he doesn't give a crap."

Abbi scratched a purring Dutchie under the chin. "Baron can't hide from me."

"Make sure she's okay. I'll find their food and load it up just in case Frankie doesn't come home today."

His chest grew heavy again. Hearing Frankie was sick had sent panic coursing through him. There was so much he hadn't told her. Like how grateful he was that she'd come into his life. He had a great relationship with Gram, but she had five boys and ten grandchildren. He'd had Frankie for himself, and when they talked each week, he was free to be himself. Not the prefect son, not the perfect one-nighter, not the fun-loving cousin. Just Cash.

He rummaged through the kitchen cabinets until he found cat food.

Did Frankie think he was ashamed of her and who his birth mom was? He'd never contacted her outside of the diner. They'd written letters back and forth when he was gone, simple letters that updated each other's on goings-on. He'd never taken her out to eat or invited her over for supper. Had Frankie ever ridden a horse? Would she?

She was less than twenty years older than his dad. She'd had Holly when she was a teenager as far as Cash knew, and she'd talked about cutting down her hours but couldn't officially retire. Dad had just turned fifty. He'd been a young twenty-two when Cash had been born. Too young for a wild man like him to settle down with a wife and kid. A kid who wasn't his wife's.

"What's wrong?" Abbi came into the kitchen, holding a disgruntled calico. She lowered Baron to the floor and the kitty scurried away.

Cash topped off the cat dishes with food and water. Abbi's gaze burned a hole in his back as he did so.

"Just thinking," he finally answered.

"You've had some curveballs thrown at you in the last twenty-four hours."

He sank back against the counter. Pressure drained from him. Abbi wasn't prying into his thoughts, but she understood.

Abbi sauntered in front of him and cupped his face. "It sucks now, but it'll be okay. It's obvious they all love you. It's them who have to learn to get along, not you who has to moderate or decide who gets your time."

She'd nailed it. He'd felt like such a traitor for *years* for associating with his own damn grandma. He'd felt like *he* was the one who'd betrayed his mom for being born, and not his dad.

Cash laid his hat on the counter and twined his arms around Abbi's waist. Heat infused her eyes and she pressed against him.

Her body against his was as good as before. Did she remember?

"Has any of that night come back to you?" he murmured.

Her lips parted and her gaze swept over his lips. "Some of it. The specifics are…fuzzy."

"Do you remember this?" He dropped his head and caught her lips. A slow press at first. She tasted better than he recalled. No beer concealed her natural flavor this time. He traced the seam of her lips with his tongue until she opened for him.

She rose to her tiptoes and snaked her arms around his neck. Their kiss deepened, and they both groaned. Blood rushed south until he considered spinning them around and stripping her down. His hands skimmed to her sides and under her sweater. Soft skin shivered with pleasure as he traced his fingers along the waist of her jeans and danced higher until they hit her bra.

Yes, this was what he needed. A bare Abbi in his hands. She moaned when he splayed his hands on her back and massaged in small circles. If she writhed against him anymore, he'd have to rip his pants off and take her on the floor.

A cat mewled. Cash ripped himself away, simultaneously pushing Abbi from his body and his growing erection.

He panted like he had to catch his breath. Dutchie meowed again and glided around their legs.

"That certainly jogged my memory." Abbi's shy smile almost undid his restraint. He'd practically thrown her off him, but she wasn't indignant, just as sweet as she tasted.

Telling her they couldn't do it again never made it out of his mouth. He couldn't recall why kissing her was a bad idea.

Because he wouldn't stop, that's why. If they had sex again, it'd be a thing between them. Then things got complicated and someone got hurt.

He snatched his hat up and launched away from the counter. "It's almost lunch. We should get our riding done before it gets too late."

What was he thinking? He wasn't as young and immature as Dad had been when he'd settled down. But if Cash started contemplating dating a girl, she couldn't be Daniels's sister. How could he ever look her parents in the eye? They'd lost a son they thought was a hero. And he had been. He'd signed his life away on the dotted line. But Daniels hadn't had to go so soon, and Cash couldn't imagine the guilt Daniels's parents would endure if they knew what had been going through their son's mind before he'd stepped into that room.

Cash strode to the front door and waited for Abbi, who said nothing about his abrupt change in attitude. He'd gone from wanting to have her for lunch to barely looking at her so he'd keep his hands off her.

They got into his truck without another word. Her phone vibrated and irritation flitted through her expression when she checked the message. She'd reacted the same way when her phone had buzzed at the hospital.

She caught him watching her and tucked her phone away. "Are you coming back to town tonight to check on Frankie?"

"Yeah, I'd better."

"Good, then I'll ride with you out to your place and come back with you. My car should be okay at the diner."

Abbi was his for the whole afternoon. She'd be stuck with him. At his mercy. After the kiss in the apartment, he doubted his ability to keep his distance. But it was better than being separated from her for now. She was a salve for his raw emotions.

~

If Cash cared for his women the way he cared for his horses, he'd win boyfriend of the year.

Abbi swayed with Mandrell's movements. She was a fine-looking creature, even if Abbi didn't know a thing about horses. Cash had chattered softly to the horses while he'd saddled them. It must soothe the creatures, but she suspected it soothed the man just as much. He'd interrupt himself to explain to Abbi what he was doing. Before he'd helped her onto Mandrell's back, Cash had shown her how to hold the reins and how to talk and move the horse.

She'd whooped—quietly—when she'd landed astride Mandrell's back without assistance.

After he had opened the gate to let them into the pasture —all while on horseback—they'd ridden out.

The land was gorgeous, even cloaked in the fading green and brown hues of autumn. Dried grasses crunched under hooves, and flocks of geese honked far above them as they began their trek south for the winter. Her stress drained away with the peaceful setting around her. She rocked with Mandrell's steps. The exhilaration of being on a horse faded to contentedness, and she understood why Cash was so dedicated to his creatures.

A herd of cattle roamed in the distance. Soft moos echoed as they munched away on what was left of green grass.

Cash pointed at them and made an arc to their left where another herd meandered. "We'll drive them to a closer pasture for the winter. It's easier to feed them and I don't have to worry about them being stranded without food and water during a blizzard."

"Does that happen often?"

"It can. Depends on the weather. You can lose several head if a freak storm hits early. The cattle freeze to death if they get separated from the rest."

"Heartbreaking."

"It is." He rested his hands on the saddle horn. Patsy Cline didn't need much guidance from him. She seemed to know his routine and what to do. His back was straight, but he rode relaxed, his boots half out of the stirrups like he'd taught her to do. "It also makes calving easier when the cattle are closer."

"Calving can be bad?"

He shot her a wry smile. "Depends on the weather. Gram used to say the true test of a marriage was how many calving seasons they survived. I've got to watch the cows for problems during birthing, and if that means checking her out every hour all night long, then that's what I do. If there's complications, I can usually deal with it without calling Bunny. Then there's the care of the calf. Is it accepted by the mom? Does the mom know what to do? Some heifers—first-time moms—get startled by their own young."

"That sucks." What a lame comment. She silently berated herself for her answer. Would he read more into it, like he was talking about his own mom?

If he read more into it, he didn't act like it. "It does. Some-times, another cow'll take over. Sometimes, she just needs a moment. If she doesn't come around, we bottle feed. If the weather's frigid, or if it's windy and snowy, then we bring them into the barn. I've caught a lucky streak the last few years and the cows haven't birthed during a major storm.

Some years, it feels like they all drop when the weather goes to hell."

"Sounds more fun than working inside all day." Even on a chilly, cloudy day when she was regretting not packing a light hat and gloves, it was invigorating being outside.

"I wouldn't trade it. If I curse getting up in the middle of the night to go out into a blizzard, all I have to do is remember having to wake up at the ass crack of dawn to work out with a bunch of smelly men. Or spending months in the desert where the days are hot and the nights get so freaking cold. Then cow shit doesn't seem so bad because it's my cattle and my place."

"Tell me how you really feel."

Cash grinned, one of his megawatt grins that tumbled through her insides. This one seemed real, not glossing over another emotion.

"Was my brother miserable?" Her abrupt subject change probably ruined the mood, but she'd come here for Perry. She couldn't forget her goal, couldn't go back home to the same old routine, minus one uptight Ellis.

Cash fell silent. The horses walked side by side.

"He was as miserable as any of us."

Abbi glared at him. "That sounds like a carefully crafted answer." She just didn't know why. If Perry had been unhappy, why not admit it?

Cash rolled a shoulder. "We all had our issues. Dealing with them far away from home, where we felt useless to the ones we love, took its toll on everyone. We all dealt with it in our own way."

"What would he feel useless about? I was in college, and Mom and Dad are Mom and Dad."

"I don't know, Abbi. Maybe he just did."

"No, I think he talked and you're not telling me." She'd grown accustomed to Cash freely chatting with her about subjects she suspected he didn't share with many other people. But when it came to her brother, his body language was tight, monitored. It was like a wall had gone up between them.

His jaw formed a hard line and he glared into the distance. The horses took step after step, lulling Abbi into almost dropping the subject.

"Would it make you feel better?" Cash finally spoke. "To know that he was worried about you? Or would you use it to wallow in self-pity?"

"I'm not like that."

"Aren't you? Have you had anyone close to you die and wonder what you could've done to change it? You came here because you felt like you didn't do enough for Daniels—Perry—so if I tell you what bothered him in the months before he died, I can't imagine you'd say, 'oh, okay,' and move on."

"It's my choice." Abbi gripped her reins firmly without tugging on Mandrell. Her curiosity and concern over Perry's last moments threatened to overwhelm her until she couldn't breathe.

"Maybe if your brother wanted you to know what he fretted over, he'd have told you."

Abbi stared at the man riding next to her. His cheeks were tinted pink from the chilly air, but he wore just a light jacket over his long-sleeved shirt. He rode as if the horse weren't even there, he and Patsy Cline so in sync. She wanted to be angry and stomp away, but she wasn't exactly in a position to do so. Why wouldn't he just talk to her? She'd used her vacation time to drive all the way up here. She'd even toasted a long-term relationship to come, but Cash didn't know that.

Perry had been plagued by personal problems when he'd

died. At least she had that confirmation. Would he have talked to her, eventually? She mulled it over.

"It was me, wasn't it? Perry was worried about me." Her throat grew thick. Of course. Perry was her older brother and he was halfway around the world while she partied all night and scraped passing grades together during the day. Her parents always hounded her about repeating failed classes because they'd raided their pension to pay for college. Had they shared their troubles with Perry?

Cash's expression turned bleak. She'd nailed it. *Oh my god.* Had Perry's concern over her been a source of distraction for him in the field? Oh god. She might've been the reason he'd made a deadly mistake.

The contents of her stomach welled up until she feared she'd hurl in front of Cash again. Would the horse panic and bolt? She had zero knowledge of what to do right now.

"Hey." Cash's voice was low as he rode closer. "You have to understand, Abbi. Brothers just worry about their sisters. We might be shit at showing our love by pointing out all the crazy plans going on in your head, but we take our role as protectors seriously. Only, when you're so far away and communication is hard, and every minute of your life is dictated by the military, it only amplifies what's banging around our heads."

Abbi cleared her throat and wiped her eyes, his words seeping in. "Yeah, I guess I can see that."

"You have to understand, too, that whatever was going on with him, it was him, not you. Don't take the way he thought and acted on yourself."

"Is there something you're not telling me?" What had Perry said? She was a selfish, irresponsible sister and should go easier on her parents?

He scowled at the space between his horse's ears. "No. He

was just a brother who was a soldier. If you're looking for anything more, it'll just lead to insanity."

She sighed, starting to think he was right. Grief had made her look too much into this. She'd had a hard enough time with Perry's death; if she took on unnecessary blame, it'd destroy her, and that'd destroy Mom and Dad. She'd made progress and that was enough for now. "Your sister drives you crazy, huh?"

"God, yes." Cash's frustrated expression remained in place. "She's so much younger than me, I feel like I was gone during her formative years. By the time I got home, she was off to college and…"

"Partying and barely passing her classes." Wryness tinted her words.

"Been there, done that?"

She chuckled. "Drove my family nuts. I was always a bit of a loose cannon. I mean, if anyone tossed out the call for a daring adventure, I was on board."

"Was?"

She nodded. "I've really grown up." She almost winced at the bitterness in her voice.

A sexy smile curved his lips. "The other night was you all grown up?"

That earned him a dirty look. "Ha-ha. No, it was more like a temporary regression."

A moment of hurt crossed his face.

"Not that I regret it," she added hastily. "I just regret the drinks I had before you joined me."

His sharp gaze pinned her, but she couldn't read his expression. When he looked away and the heat of his speculation left her, she wanted to jump over the saddle and get it back.

"Remember how to turn Mandrell?" he asked. "We'd better get back."

After they swung the horses around—and hers had noticeably picked up her pace now that home was in sight—he asked, "So what does a grown-up Abbi usually do?"

She snorted a laugh. "Boring shit." She swept her hand around them. "This is the most exciting thing I've done in years. God, I feel like I've been in prison since I graduated and got a job."

"I still say you can find work you're passionate about."

"Maybe." Not without Ellis's contribution to the bills. Now she had to pay for her own roof over her head. "But after Perry's funeral, I saw how important it was I don't heap additional stress onto my parents. I can't bring myself to disrupt what peace they've found." But at the same time, she refused to go back to the world where Ellis and Mom and Dad ran her life. No one was making decisions for her from now on. Yes, the way she'd acted in college had been immature, but not out of the ordinary for a young college woman, certainly not enough for her to sign over control of her life and the decisions she made. When Perry's life insurance paid her tuition, she couldn't throw her education away by being a precocious girl.

Coming here had been her first act as a grown-ass woman, albeit a few years too late. She couldn't go back and be the girl who never rippled the waters after this. But she'd better call Mom when she got back. They'd be mollified as long as she touched base, and it was worth being lectured that Ellis had her best interests in mind and she should listen to him.

Ignoring his texts was more power than she'd had over her life lately.

Cemented into her newfound identity, she didn't retreat into her mind for the rest of the ride. Instead, she asked more about his sister.

"She's in nursing school, taking after Mom. Well, she's

planning on nursing. She has to get into the program, and I don't know if her grades will make the cut."

"What's her backup plan?"

He let out a gusty sigh. "I doubt she has one."

Yep, worried brother. She adjusted her position in the saddle. As exhilarating as horseback riding was, her nether region wasn't used to it. Cash could probably ride for days.

His house came into sight and he muttered, "What now."

CHAPTER 9

Cash ground his teeth together as he stared at his sister's car. Abbi came to town and all hell broke loose with his family. He was caught between devoting his time to her and just using her to distance himself from the drama. But it seemed everyone was migrating to his house.

"Whose car is that?" Abbi was starting to shift and adjust in her seat. An hour and a half of riding was enough for her back end, as he'd expected.

"Sissy's." Hannah might hate that nickname, but she'd only been ten when he'd left home, so she'd stayed Sissy. "Might as well meet more of my family since you've gotten the rundown of our drama."

Hannah must've gotten the news from Dad if she'd rushed down here so fast. Mom had probably left town in the last couple of hours. Hopefully his sister wasn't crumbling under the news of the divorce. He liked to think she'd been spared from the contention in their parents' marriage.

He led them through the gate and back into the pasture the horses spent the majority of their time in.

"I wish it were under better circumstances." Abbi's brow

furrowed as she steered Mandrell, who would follow Patsy Cline anywhere, but it gave Abbi some good practice.

Cash agreed, but just like he couldn't change how he was born, he wouldn't waste time wishing things were different. Just roll with the punches like he always did.

He stopped their horses outside of the barn so they could store the tack and give the horses a quick brush. Abbi groaned as she dismounted and mimicked him as he unbuckled gear. He handed her a brush. They took more time than needed grooming their horses.

"I thought I'd find you out here." His sister's tortured voice resonated through the barn. "Oh… I didn't know you had company."

Instantly, Sissy perked up, her tears forgotten. He watched her approach over Patsy Cline's back. Sissy's gaze was riveted on Abbi as she pushed her long, brown hair behind her ears.

"I'll be nice and introduce you as Hannah," Cash said. "This is Abbi. She'd never ridden a horse before today."

Sissy smiled widely despite her red-rimmed eyes and crossed to stroke Mandrell's head. "My brother is the best one to teach you. He has a way with horses that he doesn't have with people."

"I can handle people," he mumbled.

She rolled her eyes toward them. "Yeah, but you actually like horses."

Abbi laughed. "I don't think I'm ready for any riding competitions, but it was fun."

He almost asked Sissy if she was okay, but with Abbi around, she probably wouldn't speak openly. And Abbi didn't need to deal with any more of his family's shit.

"I'm going to join the navy," Sissy announced abruptly.

Cash blinked at her in shock. "What brought that on?" She had no idea what she was getting into.

"Some asshole at school said I wouldn't get into nursing school with my grades. So fuck it, I can be a medic or something. Same thing, right?"

"No, it isn't, and you should know that before you join. And who was the asshole?"

Sissy huffed. "My college adviser. What does he know?" She squared her shoulders, her standard mutinous look on her face. "It'd give me experience and would look good on a nursing application."

"So would being a CNA, right?"

Sissy glanced away. "I got fired," she said under her breath.

Abbi watched their exchange silently. He wished the horses weren't between them, because he itched to hold her hand.

"The military might be good for you then," he said.

Sissy's surprised expression landed on him. "Seriously. You're okay with it?"

"Why wouldn't I be? It's a huge change, don't doubt that. But you'll get to experience a lot in a controlled environment. I just want you to make sure you know what you want, what's offered, and what benefits you'll get. Ask a lot of questions and take some time to decide."

His sister's demeanor lightened as his words got through to her. It'd be a miracle if she listened, but if her decision could just be a little less impulsive, he would consider it a success.

He took the lead from Abbi and led the horses back to the pasture. "How long are you staying?" he called to Sissy.

Abbi waited next to his sister, looking as comfortable as could be with her hands clenched in front of her and her gaze darting around. He liked it as much as he liked the first time he'd seen her standing in the barn's doorway.

"I...quit the semester."

Cash cringed. That was such a Sissy move.

"I have a meeting with the recruiter tomorrow."

"I'll go with." He could at least make sure she signed on the dotted line with confidence.

"Just don't tell Mom or Dad. I'll do it—later."

For once, he agreed with her. "Go fire up the grill. We'll talk over supper. Okay with you, Abbi?"

He'd call the hospital and check on Frankie while he grilled. Sissy wasn't in any shape to be alone and he didn't want to take Abbi back to town so soon—or at all tonight. Leaving her with Sissy was just poor hospitality on his part. And who knew what trouble Sissy would cook up while he was gone. Hell, what would she do while he was there?

Abbi and Sissy laughed in the kitchen. They'd gotten so loud, he'd had a hard time hearing Frankie. She was doing better but didn't know when she'd get released. Knowing she was in good hands took some weight off his shoulders as he finished supper. He stopped before he went inside, the plate of steaks steaming in his hand.

Sissy was giggling as she and Abbi chopped tomatoes and cucumbers for a salad. Abbi waved around the knife, telling some story he couldn't hear.

The doubts he'd had his entire life about his chances for a family diminished with the sight. Why couldn't he make a girl happy? He wasn't Dad. He wasn't geared toward cheating. At least, he didn't think he was. He hadn't been in a relationship long enough to try. Except for some dating in high school with copious amounts of warnings to *treat her right* and *don't break her heart* from Mom, he'd given up trying.

You're just like your dad. But Mom never said that in regard to women. She said it every time he rode at a breakneck speed to chase down a loose bull. He heard it during cattle drives when they coaxed a hundred head of cattle into another pasture. Or when he fooled around and stood up in the saddle. People told him he was just like his dad when they saw the two of them standing together. But he wasn't his dad. Why had that dawned on him just now?

Maybe…maybe he could…explore this thing with Abbi. Because when he was with her, he knew no other woman. He hadn't once thought about heading out to get laid. And if he thought about sex, or anything leading up to the act, it was Abbi he wanted.

"Dude, do you see a ghost?" Sissy called through the door. "I knew this place was haunted. I mean, it's only Gramps. Probably. It'd be creepy if it weren't. Wait—it'd be creepy if it were."

Abbi's stiffened and she squinted into each corner.

He stepped in to finish supper preparations. "Gramps didn't pass away here," he clarified.

"But his spirit is tied to the place." Sissy bounced toward the dining room with a dish of potato salad in her hands. "There are worse people to haunt you, just saying."

"The house isn't haunted." Cash crowded next to Abbi; she didn't move away. "But Sissy's right. He was pretty protective of us when he was alive."

"Just no summonings, please," Abbi said, "or I'm walking home."

He chuckled and bent to kiss her neck. She jumped and he nipped harder. His body roared to life.

Not now. He embraced all the discipline he could muster. Just because he'd had the epiphany he could maybe think about having a girlfriend without making her miserable, it didn't mean Abbi was the one. Starting a relationship with secrets was a good way to hurt her.

She slid him a wicked smile that tangled up his insides and picked up her lettuce salad. She winked. "Nice meat."

He chuckled and followed her into the dining room with his platter of steaks.

The meal was like their normal family get-togethers, the good ones when no one was irate with anyone else. Sissy told stories about her barrel-riding days and Abbi's interest seemed genuine, not feigned, unlike most people when Sissy got started on her passion.

Then somehow, the topic turned to the pranks Cash and his cousins played on each other. They'd started out putting hay in each others' hats, then grown to moving trucks to the other side of the field when they were out working. Abbi roared with laughter at a retelling of the time Aaron drove the yard mower to town to go through the drive-thru at the burger joint. He'd only been sixteen and his parents hadn't been thrilled when the cops had given them a courtesy call.

She added a few of her own with Perry. Cash tried to relax while hearing the stories of her brother. Perry sounded much more carefree than the soldier Cash had known.

Sissy pushed her plate away and plopped her elbows on the table. "I bet you two are close."

Cash tensed. Oh shit, they'd never told Sissy who exactly Abbi was.

"Yeah, we were." She passed Sissy a sad smile. "He was killed in action almost three years ago."

A myriad of emotions crossed Sissy's face. A mix of confusion, horror, and remorse. "I'm so sorry."

Abbi waved her off. "It was really nice, actually, to talk about him without everyone going all gushy eyed and serious." She took a pull off her beer. "It's like at home, my parents use his death as a reminder, like a constant lesson. They don't want to lose me, too."

"Your parents ride your ass about being an adult? So

hypocritical." Sissy shook her head, brown hair flying. "Like I don't notice that they don't have their shit together, either."

"Sissy!" Nothing like airing dirty laundry in front of his guest. It was different when he confided to her, but to hang it out there at the dinner table?

"I know, right?" Abbi talked over him. "I feel like it's a lot of pressure. Like I'm the hinge that's keeping it all together."

Cash reclined in this chair while the girls had a major bonding moment. He'd never felt like he was keeping the family together, quite the opposite. He'd always held the blame for tearing his parents apart. The adult part of his brain knew his thought process as a kid wasn't logical, that Dad was to blame—but did it matter?

This conversation wasn't about him, though. Sissy had someone who understood, which was something he could never give her.

His gaze danced between them as they faced each other, talking with their hands and punctuating sentences with "dude."

Then Sissy slammed her hand on the table, jerking his attention off Abbi's twinkling hazel eyes. "Seriously? You haven't?"

"I've been fishing, I just haven't caught anything."

Sissy snapped her fingers and circled her hand in the air like she was rounding them up. "Grab the gear, Cash. We need to fix this."

Abbi giggled as she shucked her shoes. When was the last time she'd had this much fun? And alcohol wasn't involved. Good, clean entertainment.

She eyed the shore of the lake. Brown, crusty cattails

grew in patches. Shriveled weeds and grass lined the shore, along with a few feet of mud.

Clean wasn't in the cards tonight. She rolled up her pants as far as she could, which was only to her shins.

"The water's going to be cold." Cash spread out gear on a gigantic rock that made a perfect table. "You can use the rocks to fish from. That's what we usually do; it's why we piled them here."

"Where in the world did you find huge rocks like this? Did you buy them?"

Sissy chuckled. "We cleaned them out of the fields."

Different world. Her grandparents had likely done the same thing, but she'd been too young to care about the logistics. She straightened with a grin and studied the shore. "Bet I can get closer like this."

Hannah was already rolling her jeans. "Great minds think alike. We need to immerse ourselves in the process."

Abbi tiptoed to Cash. The fresh smell of the lake draped over her. What would it be like to have full access to a place like this? She could come out here and sit, not stress about ex-boyfriends or how her parents were reacting to the breakup. She could perch on a rock and soak up sunbeams, just because. Watch Cash fish, watch his muscles flex and bunch as he cast. But what she'd anticipate, what she'd study for hours, was that look of calm on his face. When he relaxed fully, when he seemed at peace, Abbi wanted to draw him. The real Cash. How many people saw him like that?

"Abbi?"

Oops. Too much staring, not enough listening. "I didn't hear. Say it again?"

He handed her a fishing pole.

She accepted it, giddiness warming her body. "Is that a marshmallow?"

"Cheap bait for stocked trout." Hannah bounced to the

rock and lifted her rod. "Kinda like cheating, but better than driving fifteen miles one way to the nearest public lake."

"So this should be a gimme." She picked her way through the mud. Cold, squishy earth stuck between her toes.

"Go, go, go, go." Hannah had already chosen her spot and cast.

Cash hauled himself up to the rock and stood to cast. "A gimme doesn't mean I'm cleaning your fish for you."

After a few minutes, the end of Abbi's rod jerked. "I got one, I got one." She tried jumping up and down as she reeled it in, but her feet were stuck in the mud. She waved her arm for balance, but fell backward.

Hannah laughed, but by the time Abbi's butt hit the ground, Cash was by her side. He handed the rod off to his sister and held out a hand for Abbi.

"My fish!" Abbi got out between laughs. Ice water seeped through her pants and she was covered in muck.

She clasped Cash's warm hand. He popped her up, steadying her with another hand at her waist.

"Don't worry." He held her. "Hannah's got it for you to reel in after you stand up."

He walked her to Hannah's side. She had laid her own rod down and presented hers.

Abbi brought the fish in with Cash murmuring encouragement in her ear. Her face had to be split from ear to ear with her grin. His soothing voice, his hands on her. A beautiful, wiggling trout hanging off her line.

They hung around to fish for another hour before she started shivering too badly. Abbi would've gutted it out, but Hannah's teeth were chattering and Cash was constantly shooting her and his sister worried looks.

Cleaning the fish was even fun.

"You'll have to let me cook these for you." Abbi bit her lip after the words left her mouth. Was that too presumptuous?

She wanted to come back, or stay—either way, she didn't want this to end.

"Of course." Cash loaded their gear and spread out a towel in the passenger seat of his pickup for her to sit on. "The full experience is what Sissy promised you."

Hannah crawled into the back after wiping her feet off the best she could. "And it's what you're gonna get."

As they drove back, Abbi looked herself over. A muddy mess, though much of it dried. Ellis would've shit himself if she'd walked up to his vehicle in the state she was in. As if he'd be out fishing in less than a boat, a life vest, and white sunblock slathered on his nose.

The towel Cash spread out for her was an old one he must keep on hand, but he only had one and Hannah sat in the back with grimy feet. Abbi's feet were in worse shape, with nothing between them and the floor mat.

"It'll dry and vacuum out easy enough," Cash said. "This truck has seen much worse."

"I was just marveling that I wouldn't get away with this at home, and your vehicle is more expensive than anything I've been in before."

"It's just a pickup. We treat our equipment with respect, but it's purchased with work in mind. Getting dirty is a part of life."

"It's a part of your life. But I was messing around."

"Oh, we mess around, honey." Cash's eyes twinkled with mischief.

"I'm going to ignore the innuendo," Hannah said, "and agree with Cash. There's no reason to feel guilty. Live a little."

Words she used to live by. Live a little. She could pinpoint exactly when she'd quit living. Three weeks after she'd buried her brother, she'd been asked out by her girlfriends. She'd called Ellis, and he'd asked her what her parents would think, pointed out that she should consider their feelings.

Emotion swelled, a mixture Abbi couldn't identify. Loss, bitterness, regret. She'd have to deal with those, but not tonight.

Hannah tapped her shoulder. "You're staying longer, right? We can find you something to wear."

"Oh, I don't know—"

"Come on. It's so early yet. Like, not even ten p.m."

Her mind spun. She wanted to say yes so badly. And not just to be around Cash longer. With Hannah, she'd found the thrill of life she'd been missing.

"Oh, wait. Cash?" Hannah cocked her head to the side. "I think I heard her say yes. Did you hear her say yes?"

Abbi giggled and Cash grinned. She recognized the signs. Big brother couldn't say no to little sister. How many times had Perry caved to her shenanigans? He might have regretted it after they'd been busted by their parents, like when Abbi was ten and had filled Mom's expensive vases with sand and earth worms.

"Do you mind?" she asked Cash.

"Ain't nothing better than a midnight fish fry, honey."

Abbi was breathless. She fanned herself and gasped in lungfuls of air. She sank into the couch as her last fit of laughter died down. Her stomach was ready to burst from all the food she'd eaten in the last hour and the empty cans of beer littered in front of her.

They were in the basement. Cash had the fireplace going, but Abbi would've been warm enough in his old, gray army sweatshirt and flannel bottoms borrowed from his sister. Her feet were bare, but toasty, and shoved under the couch cushions, where Cash's butt warmed them.

Hannah abruptly rose and stretched. "I have a meeting with the recruiter tomorrow, and since it's one in the morning, I'm getting my ass to bed."

Cash opened his mouth, but Hannah flounced up the stairs, leaving them alone. Abbi considered her environment. She was sitting alone with him, with her feet under his ass. The night was ending on a high note.

"Well, then," he said and patted her leg. "It's going to be an early morning. Mom always cleans up after herself, so the room she used is ready to go for you."

"Okay. Thanks." Disappointment curdled in her belly. What had she expected?

A whole lot more. She'd just spent hours bonding with him and his sister and he'd taught her how to cook a damn good fillet.

He stood and held out a hand for her. She unfolded herself and accepted it.

But when she rose, he didn't move. And she was close. A subtle smell of lake and savory seasonings clung to him. A little smudge of flour from breading the fish clung to his black T-shirt.

Her hand was still in his. She licked her lips and gazed up at him.

Heat filled his eyes, but he didn't make a move.

Her attention dropped to his lips. He was a good kisser. She liked that about him. She liked a lot about him. Releasing his hand, she rested hers on his shoulders.

"I'm not touching you tonight, Abbi," he said softly.

Startled, she met his gaze. "Why not?"

She had to ask why a guy didn't want her. Humiliation started a slow burn in her cheeks.

His gaze swept the empty drink cans around them. He

dropped his head to whisper in her ear. "Because the next time we have sex, you're going to remember every second."

Hot desire replaced embarrassment. She wanted that, too.

So many retorts ran through her head, but she didn't know what to say.

Finally, she playfully pushed him away. "You should've told me earlier. Now we both have to wait."

Shooting him her most sultry smile, she sauntered up the stairs.

CHAPTER 10

Cash woke up early to do chores. With a groan, he got out of bed and dressed. Too little sleep. That sexy woman in the next room was messing up his schedule left and right.

He pulled on a hoodie over his shirt. Early October mornings could either be refreshing or cold as fuck depending on what the wind and sun wanted to do.

He went toward the kitchen. His nose twitched.

Toast?

He ambled into the kitchen and stopped. The best ass he'd ever seen was turned toward him as Abbi spread peanut butter and jelly onto some bread.

Were those his boxers?

Yeah, he'd probably stashed some clothes he didn't wear anymore but hadn't gotten rid of in the room Mom had used. He was horrible about caring for the house and everything inside. He'd much rather be out doing his chores, working cattle, and riding horse.

Unless this was inside waiting for him. Abbi's round butt cheeks bunched and flexed as she reached for more toast.

When she popped back on her heels, her butt bounced and filled his head with ideas of what she looked like as he took her from behind.

Auburn hair swung from a messy ponytail. She was an ultimate temptress without trying.

As if getting to sleep with a raging erection hadn't been a hard enough challenge, he had to do chores while his shaft throbbed and cursed him for having too much pride. Who cared how clearly she remembered their time together as long as she was willing?

He cared.

His gut told him she hadn't been hammered and the sex would've been more phenomenal than before. But he'd been blindsided by her nearly complete lack of recall last time. A night that'd rocked his world had left her in the dark.

But today was a new day. He tapped on the doorframe.

She spun with a gasp. "Oh god, you scared me."

"Couldn't sleep?"

She winced, but covered it with a chuckle. "I must be too used to slamming hotel doors. It's like the complete silence out here is so loud. It takes some getting used to and I'll totally need a nap later." Handing him a plate of toast, her smile almost shy. "We ate so late last night, I wasn't sure you'd want anything, but I need a little something in my stomach."

"Oh, good. I thought your reaction the other day was from me."

Pink colored her cheeks. "I think it had more to do with the greasy food I piled onto the alcohol from the night before."

He bit into his toast.

"You make my body feel other things."

He almost choked and she snickered.

He finished his food and dug out a couple glasses for juice. "You remember last night, though?"

Shooting him a meaningful look, she accepted her glass of OJ. "Yes. I didn't have that much to drink, and I didn't mix alcohol."

So, he'd missed his chance. But he wanted to hear his name screamed from her lips and Sissy was staying under the same roof. Awkward.

Abbi wasn't going to be another quick fuck. Last time hadn't turned out quick, either, thanks to him conking out like a baby until morning.

"Are you going back to bed or getting your hands dirty with me?" He held his breath, waiting for her answer. Spending this much time with a woman who wasn't kin just didn't happen, but he wanted it to.

She peered out the kitchen window and looked down at her clothes. "I'll run and change."

The corner of his mouth kicked up in a smile, and he made sure not to miss her sexy sashay out of the room.

He stayed in place and stared down into his glass.

He liked her. Despite her reason for hanging around him, the part of her brother she hadn't known, she'd been the calm in the storm that was his family life the last few days.

There'd been no abuse, so Cash had always justified his parents' relationship and how they treated him as normal. He was lucky—he had a home, he was his own boss, and his family loved him. And Mom did love him, even though they didn't share blood. There'd been no cruelty. His father had never raised a hand to Mom or Sissy. Neither had Mom physically punished Cash or Sissy. Groundings had been fairly frequent and Mom could give a tongue-lashing that'd leave a man limping but nothing close to corporal punishment.

So, he'd told himself he had it good. Damn good. But he

just wasn't cut out for a relationship—he was his father's son, after all.

He frowned as he remembered the time in high school when he'd started dating Bobbi Jo Wilkins. They'd been sixteen and she'd been the cheerleader for his football team. Things had been going well, drama free, and Bobbi Jo had gone through the meet-the-parents gig. He and Bobbi Jo hadn't even had sex, both still virgins despite some hot and heavy make-out sessions.

Then he'd been waiting for a ride after school. Mom was going to pick him up because she'd had to use the truck that day. Waiting outside, he'd been laughing and joking around with Jennie, another classmate. Didn't think it'd even elevated to the level of harmless flirting.

But Mom had seen and been pissed. He'd gotten lectured all the way home about how he didn't deserve a nice girl like Bobbi Jo if he couldn't refrain from hitting on another girl at only sixteen. Mom had asked him to imagine how Bobbi Jo would've felt driving up on a scene like that and then having to walk around school the next day while everyone gave her pitying looks.

Cash had been humbled and guilt ridden. He'd broken up with Bobbi Jo the next day, thinking he was doing her a favor. She was married now, with three kids, and still one of the sweetest people he knew. But he'd changed that day.

God, why hadn't he seen it? He didn't get a case of what-could-have-beens when he thought of his first and last official girlfriend, but that day had changed the whole trajectory of his life.

His time with Abbi made him ask what would've happened if he'd stayed in a relationship at sixteen. Cheating wasn't inevitable. Sure, he'd been a teenager at the mercy of his hormones, had found other girls attractive, but he hadn't once considered so much as kissing anyone other than Bobbi Jo.

As far as he knew, his uncles had never cheated. Cash had grown up with them as father figures as much as his own.

It was a lot to think about.

"Ready?" Abbi bounded back in. Her hair remained in a messy ponytail, but she wore her clothes from the previous day, only freshly laundered.

"I'll get my boots."

He led her to the side of the barn where the tractor sat with the feeder attachment already hooked and filled. Slowing, he eyed the setup.

"I didn't mention," he glanced at her, "that it's not a two-seater."

"So… I run behind you or what?"

It was hard to get her worked up. He liked that about her. "I can show you how to drive, or you can stand and hang on."

He expected a dubious, *Are you kidding?* Riding shotgun was something he and his cousins had always done. The safety police would've had a heart attack if they'd seen how the kids would plant their feet on one of the steps and hold on as huge wheels turned in front and behind them.

She clapped her hands and jumped up and down. "I'll hang on and watch you drive first. Then I'll take over. I don't want to run over any cows."

He hopped in and fired it up, then showed Abbi where to grip. Fighting the smile on his face proved impossible as she oohed and aahed over everything.

"This is so beautiful." She whipped her head around, her cheeks pink from the chilly breeze, tendrils of hair licking her face. "I bet it's gorgeous in the summer, all green and full of wildflowers. Ohmigosh, is that a hawk? It's huge!" She released a gusty sigh. "I miss this. I didn't get to help

Grandpa much because I was too young, but I can remember playing in the fields."

She chatted and asked questions about what they were doing. Cash flat-out laughed at her excitement over filling the troughs with feed.

"Look at that!" She practically danced on her perch. "It just shoots out from that wagon-thingy and—*boom!* Cows are fed."

He normally enjoyed his morning chores. They'd become a comforting routine, a way to reconnect with the basics of life. He had a job, healthy cows, fertile bulls, and was surrounded by family. But Abbi's presence and exuberance showed that maybe, just maybe, he'd been a little lonely.

"Are we done?" Abbi didn't sound like she wanted it to be over.

"Way more cattle, honey."

"I'll drive on the way back."

Abbi's fatigue drained away. The sun was peeking out behind thin clouds, cows meandered across the field for breakfast, and the drone of the tractor wasn't unpleasant.

Suck it, Ellis. His incessant texts had woken her up early. If she'd continued sleeping, she would've missed this.

How exhilarating.

She'd left her phone on silent in the guest bedroom. The day was hers—early morning fresh air, no one but her and a hot rancher.

Thank you, Ellis.

Cash maneuvered the tractor across an expanse of pasture that had tire tracks and paralleled the dirt road that ran past his house.

She leaned in. "Where are we going?"

"To the bull pasture. We keep them separate from the cows." He slid her an amused look. "After they're done fuckin'."

"How scandalous! You said you were bringing them into the stockyard around the barn for the winter. What do you do with the bulls when they can't, you know, fraternize?"

"We drive them over to Travis's house. I can't give 'em enough room in my place."

"Drive?"

"Gate."

Drive a gate? She followed Cash's gaze. Oh. Abbi playfully scowled at him before she jumped down and opened the metal gate between pastures. Cash idled through and stopped to wait for her.

"We could load them up into a trailer and literally drive them over," he explained, "but it's easier to take the horses and herd them. It's not far." He flashed her the panty-melting grin she lived for. Only this time, his eyes were fully engaged, too. "And it's fun as hell."

"A real cattle drive. Awesome." So much better than counting someone else's money all day.

She was in the wrong profession. Could she change it? What would her parents think if she came home and told them she was done at the bank?

No, they'd want her to have an alternate in place first. What else could she do? Sell her sketches at a street fair?

Shoving her worries away, she lifted her face to the sun. The temperature had risen, promising another vibrant Midwest autumn day.

They wrapped up feeding and Cash stopped the tractor.

"Your turn."

They switched spots without her jumping down and it involved his hands on her hips and getting really close. She flushed, and it had nothing to do with the sunshine.

Last night, she'd been close to him, too. It messed with a girl's mind. She had never felt that flustered around a man or been that…anticipatory. The feeling amassed the longer she was around him. The commitment-phobe player loved his family hard, was passionate about his work, and treated her like…herself.

She didn't want to go back home. Never mind the mess with Ellis and either finding her own place or moving back in with her parents. She didn't want to go back and deal with any of it. She had no desire to return to her boring, plain life.

And today, she didn't have to worry about it.

She settled into the seat warm with Cash's body heat. She'd rather be personally enveloped in his heat. "Okay, what now?"

"Have you ever driven a stick shift?"

She scanned the dash and levers. "Absolutely. My high school car was a standard."

"Well, it's kind of like that, but you have a throttle."

He ran through the explanation, and after a few jerks and lurches, she was cruising along with Cash standing on the side.

"This is so fun!" She wasn't going very fast, but she doubted she'd have more fun driving a race car. Once they crossed the pasture, she stopped the tractor. "Gate."

His eyes sparkling with humor, he jumped down and opened the gate. When he clambered back on, she grinned and rolled through.

"Now what?" she asked.

"I could introduce you to the world of fixing fences, but Sissy has her meeting with the recruiter and I need a shower first." He paused for a moment. "I can take you back to town or you can hang out at the house."

She mentally beamed at his offer, but she'd be alone at his place with nothing to do but miss him and feel like a freeloader. "I can grab a fresh pair of clothes in town, and I'd love to check on Frankie and her place."

A glow of surprise lit his eyes. "Sure. I planned to stop by after the recruiter."

"Pick me up from the hotel before you go? I owe you lunch this time and I never got to try that omelet."

"It's a date, honey."

Abbi brushed through her hair, smiling to herself about her sort-of date with Cash. She looked forward to it more than a legit date. Going with Cash to check on Frankie and her cats meant more than any *are we going to hook up or not* date.

What a vacation. It was meant to be for soul-searching, getting answers about her brother's last moments on earth, and she'd done both, in a way.

Mental peace spread through her as she reconciled how she felt with the circumstances of Perry's death. Maybe she'd been bothered because she hadn't known anyone he was with, but Cash didn't seem like the type of guy that'd let the army lie about her brother getting killed. She was thinking too Hollywood; this was reality.

As for soul-searching, just coming here without Ellis was a huge step to finding herself. She hadn't been Abbi Daniels for the last three years. After their first year together, when her world had crashed, she'd been Ellis's girlfriend—behaving how he and her parents wanted. Around Cash, and even Hannah, she'd been fully accepted as reckless Abbi.

Go fishing in cold water? Sure. Fish fry at midnight? Let's do it. Gotta get up early? Who cares! One night without eight hours of sleep didn't make her impetuous.

There was a knock on the door. She dropped her brush and raced out of the bathroom.

Cash was early. She flung open the door without checking the peephole.

His tired smile warmed her as much as his charming grin. He was wearing his navy blue Walker Five ball cap and a tan jacket that looked like it had come out of a cowboy catalog, which made sense. As a farmer and rancher, Cash was part cowboy.

"The recruiter didn't take as long as I had hoped."

She stepped back to let him in. From the subtle strain hidden in his expression, the meeting must not have gone well. "You wanted it to take longer?"

He stepped inside and bypassed the horribly uncomfortable desk chair to drop onto the edge of the bed. "Much longer. Ask some questions, find out what kind of benefits she can get depending on what job she chooses. Find out length of training, what it entails, where she could get stationed…" He blew out a breath. "Damn, just find out more. Instead, we walk in and she asks about being a nurse and learns she'd have to finish nursing school, so she says, 'What about a medic?' He gives her his spiel and she smiles and nods, sets up a time to go to the processing center to join. I tried asking some basic questions and she kicked me out."

"She's joining the navy, huh?"

"'Going to see the world.'" He glared at the floor between his boots.

Worry for his sister radiated off him. He needed comfort. She sank down next to him and curled her arm through his, resting her head on his shoulder.

"I'm not against her joining, just with being so impulsive."

Abbi bristled. Was impulsiveness only bad in sisters? Hadn't Cash ever made sudden decisions based on little information? Perry had—and he'd always gotten away with it. "You don't like that trait in her?"

"Not when it's her future." His forehead creased, but he wrapped an arm around her. "I don't want her to have a ton of regrets, thinking she should've stayed in school, then joined as an officer and made more money. Or realizing she hates anything medical and wishing she'd joined as a…a… I don't fucking know."

"Or she might find out it was the perfect decision and be really happy."

"I hope so." He didn't sound convinced.

Abbi tipped her chin up to meet his gaze. "You aren't responsible for her happiness. She's an adult and she's in charge. Sometimes the best thing a brother can do is accept his sister just the way she is."

The corners of his eyes crinkled with his smile. "You sound like you speak from experience."

She straightened but managed to stay in his embrace. "Honestly, if I had been allowed to make hasty decisions about my future, I think I would've been happier. Instead, I majored in what would make everyone else happy. I got a job that was expected of me. I've done nothing with my life that my younger self would've wanted and I'm miserable. Perry was the only one I could talk to about any of it. He accepted me the way I was."

Cash gazed at her for a few heartbeats, his expression solemn. "He worried about you."

Her heart twisted. She should've pretended everything was peachy the few times he was able to call.

"Hey," Cash said softly. "What's wrong?"

"I shouldn't have stressed him."

His face hovered inches from hers. "He would've anyway. It's what we do."

She wasn't letting Cash get away this time. Stretching up, she kissed him. He didn't tense or pull away but hugged her closer, like it was what he needed, too.

Pulling his hat off, she dropped it behind him and snuggled closer. Combined with his efforts, she ended up straddling his lap.

Her lips parted. Their tongues danced and licked at each other, but their hands stayed firmly in place. Odd. She'd been ready to strip down the second he walked in, but this closeness filled an empty hole inside of her. One she'd had no idea existed. He confided in her, didn't hold back when he would have with others. It was the emotional equality she'd been craving in a relationship.

He splayed his hands on her back and squeezed her to him as they devoured each other. The hard length of him pressed into her, a decadent tease that heightened the pleasure of being in his arms.

Grinding into him, she managed some restraint and reached for the promise that they'd be like this soon, only with no clothes. And when the time was right.

Because he wasn't reaching up her striped blouse, or trying to undo her skinny jeans, he must need this connection, too. They kissed and hugged, kind of like getting to know each other without words.

Until his jacket started to vibrate.

He paused and they broke apart.

"Is that a phone in your pocket or are you happy to see me?" She didn't move from his lap, had no wish to.

Heat simmered in his gaze, his expression intent. "Oh, I'm happy to see you."

Capturing her mouth again, they continued where they'd left off and his phone went silent. Finally, his hands drifted down to the hem of her shirt. Warm fingers hit her back and she sighed into him. This was going to be good.

His phone started vibrating again.

With a frustrated chuckle, she rolled off his lap onto the bed. "You'd better answer."

He snatched his phone from his coat and glowered at the screen. "What now?"

Abbi saw "Dad" on the screen before Cash put the phone to his ear.

"Yeah?" Cash's gaze swept her body, but he glanced away as she heard a man's voice, though she couldn't make out the words. "No." Pause. "Went back home yesterday. I doubt she's answering your calls. Can you blame her?" Cash rested his elbows on his thighs and dropped his head into his free hand. "No, Mom seemed all right. Except…" A heavy sigh. "I told her that Frankie was in the hospital and I was helping her out." Pause. "Yes, Holly's mom—my grandma." There was an edge to his voice. "Look, I'll try calling and, yes, Sissy is here and she's fine, too."

Abbi raised a brow, but Cash didn't spill to his dad what his sister was up to.

He disconnected and passed her an apologetic look. "Dad can't get ahold of Mom."

He punched in a number and put the phone back to his ear.

"Mom? What's going on? Dad said he can't reach you."

Patty's angry voice floated through the phone, but again Abbi couldn't make out the words. She hated eavesdropping, but there was nowhere else to go and he could've gone into the hallway. He hadn't. Did that mean he didn't mind her hearing? She stretched out on the bed, honored he wasn't going into hiding. He must trust her, or at least trust that she could handle it. He hadn't seemed like the type to share the intricacies of his life or anyone else's.

Had Perry entrusted Cash with any secrets? Would he share with her, or think he was protecting her? She might have to talk with him about that. Not only was that why she was here, but after what they'd gone through together, his openness with her would make secrecy on this subject feel like a betrayal.

"You're staying *where*?" His sudden heat yanked her attention back. "Who? Is he a—" his shoulders slumped, "—boyfriend?"

She sat up. Astonishment flooded his face, followed by dismay.

"Not at all. You deserve to be happy. Of course, I understand. It just seems so sudden."

"I've been unhappy for almost thirty years," Patty's voice cast through the phone clearly. "When I met someone who actually respected me, I decided to get to know him."

His shoulders drooped farther. "I know. I'll just text Dad and tell him you're okay."

She clasped her hands on her lap. How often had he played mediator between his mom and dad? That was no role for a child, no matter what age.

How often had he shouldered the blame for the circumstances behind his birth?

CHAPTER 11

Cash finished sending the message to Dad.

A draft cooled his now-empty lap. Abbi was quiet next to him. A muscle flexed in his jaw. Heaven had surrounded him and his duties had faded away. For all of a minute.

His responsibilities rushed back. He had to check on Frankie, her cats, call his sister for details.

Abbi's lush body curved into him. "I'm sorry."

He draped an arm over her shoulders, her presence chasing away a few pounds of pressure. "Thanks."

His parents had never apologized to him, but she had within minutes of seeing what it was like for him.

"Your mom's found someone new?"

He dipped his head. The news wasn't sitting well with him. What had happened to his normal dysfunctional family? Less than forty-eight hours ago, he'd learned his parents were divorcing and his mom had already moved in with someone. His dad could be, too! Sissy was running off to the military, leaving just him, doing as she'd always done.

"Do you think Hannah knows?" she asked.

He didn't even want to contemplate that. "No, and she's going to go nuclear when she finds out."

"What's she going to do—run off and join the navy?"

Cash barked out a laugh. "Good point."

Abbi slipped away from him and stood. She held out her hand. "But you know what? Your mom can tell her. It's not your job."

Easier said than done. Sissy just took bad information better from him. All those years Mom and Dad wouldn't speak to each other, she'd turned to him. In a weird way, helping Sissy helped him process what was going on.

Abbi wiggled her fingers. His lips twitched into a smile. She was right. He clasped her hands and rose.

She looked up at him. "By the way, I'm taking you out to eat tonight."

A grudging smile played on his lips. "Are you sure you don't want to fish in the cold mud and have another fish fry?"

"I absolutely want to do that again. But it's my turn to provide food."

"Come on." He dropped his tone low. "I've got some pussy waiting for me."

Laughter bubbled from her. "I don't doubt it. After being alone all night, Dutchie and Baron will rub all up and down you."

They both swapped pussy jokes on the way out to his truck and to Frankie's place, and the juvenile humor was just the levity he'd been looking for. He let them inside Frankie's tiny apartment. He'd expected the cats to swarm them, but her apartment stayed quiet and the cats remained aloof. Abbi went to check on them while he dished out the cat food. She hadn't come back into the kitchen yet. If something happened to those furballs on his watch... He went searching and found her looking at the pictures on the wall.

If he were honest, it was something he'd wanted to do the last time they were here.

"You look like her," Abbi murmured.

He glanced at the picture of Holly on her graduation day. She was blond and blue-eyed, too. He looked and acted like his dad, and he shared his birth mom's nose and smile.

"Yeah," was all he said. Whenever he thought of Holly, he didn't get angry or resentful. He brimmed with sadness, not for himself, but for a young woman who went through life so unhappy that she had to end it herself.

"I'm sorry. Are you okay?" Abbi touched his face.

His brows drew down. "Yeah. Why?"

"You seem sad. Do you ever wonder…?"

He shook his head. "I don't think about it, honestly. She didn't want me." That came out harsher than intended. "Maybe she did and was too overwhelmed." He shrugged. "She had problems." That was as much as he ever let himself think about it.

"You feel sorry for her?"

He blew out a breath. "I do. But…" He swallowed. God, was he really going to say this? "I wonder sometimes if my lack of emotion when it comes to my birth mother stems from not wanting to hurt Mom by thinking about her. So, I try to just hope that she found some peace in life, and I really do know that she did the best thing she could for me. Life with her would've been…turbulent."

She cupped his face in both hands; he stared into her shimmering hazel eyes. "You have such a good heart for the people around you who've hurt you."

Hurt him? "What do you mean?"

"You haven't done a damn thing wrong, but all the adults in your life have swept you along in their personal drama. Yet you worry about them and care for them." She brushed her lips against his.

When she pulled away, he expected her face to be full of sympathy, steeled himself for it, but her small smile was almost shy.

Keys jiggled in the front door. They both turned to face it, not knowing what to expect.

Frankie trudged in, wearing her black work shirt and black slacks. The clothing she'd worn to the hospital.

He rushed to her side. "You busted out. Why didn't you call?"

She jumped, her hand flying to her heart. Dear lord, he wasn't giving his grandma a heart attack, was he?

"Cash, hello. Oh, and Abbi." She relaxed, her expression pleased. "I can see my darlings were well cared for. You didn't have to stop by today, too."

"We wanted to." He guided her to a chair. "How'd you get home?"

"Called a cab." Frankie settled into a chair with a sigh that said she didn't want to move any time soon.

"Why the hell did you do that?" There was no heat in his words. Frankie was too damn independent and too intent not to intrude in Cash's life, she would've never entertained the idea of asking him for help.

While Frankie got settled, Abbi went into the kitchen. Since they had a moment of privacy, he decided to make sure Frankie knew she'd never be intruding.

"Look, I told Mom and Dad that I see and talk to you regularly. So don't worry that contacting me will upset anything. We're family."

Surprise flitted through her face and her eyes glistened. She patted his hand. "You're such a good boy. I was so upset at myself for passing out Monday morning because it meant I missed my time with you."

"Well, then," he drawled, "we may have to implement a weekly dinner night." He smirked at Abbi as she exited the kitchen with a glass of water for Frankie. "I hear I cook a mean fish fillet."

Abbi handed the glass off to Frankie. His grandma seemed both pleased and uncomfortable with the attention.

"He mans a wicked grill, too." Abbi sat on the couch, probably so it didn't seem like they were hovering over her.

He sat next to her. "If you're back at work next week, we'll set a date."

Frankie's eyes softened the way Gram's did when he and his cousins did something sweet. It was the first time he'd compared Frankie to Gram. Frankie was Frankie, technically his grandma, but she'd been at arm's length for the last few years. Almost nonexistent before that. Gram was the stereo-typical grandmother. She'd diapered him, chased after him, shamelessly spoiled him. He even lived in her old house.

Now, as the three of them chatted and talked about doctor's orders and going back to work and the history of the fat cats roaming around and what plants did the best indoors, Frankie was more than his birth mom's mom. She was his family.

They walked out of Frankie's place to Cash's truck. The cool autumn breeze wasn't unpleasant and the sun was still warm enough to ward off the worst of the chill.

"Is it too early for supper?" Abbi had missed lunch but wanted to get to the dessert. She and Cash had grown closer; it wreaked havoc on her hormones. Had she ever wanted a man more than she wanted Cash?

Sure, she remembered brief glimpses of their first night together, but it was dulled from the haze of alcohol. But then it'd been all crazy attraction and finally letting herself run amok. Now, it was…more.

He sighed regretfully. "I might grab a bite, but I have some fences to mend before we move cattle." He lifted a shoulder as if in apology. "The guys are planning to help me bring cattle in a couple of weeks, so I have to get everything ready."

"I can still hang onto my promise of supper. Keep the door unlocked and I'll bring groceries over and cook you something." Her smile felt frozen in place. Was he going to refuse? She had zero desire to go back to her empty hotel room and sit around, ignoring Ellis's texts and calls.

His eyes twinkled. "I can't promise my oven works after a summer of grilling." He helped her into the pickup, which was unnecessary, but she'd never complain about his hands on her. "How 'bout we stop and get groceries before we head back?"

She met his gaze. He was asking her to sleep over. The part of her that she'd allowed to have too much say in her life begged her to take things slower, to remember her life back home had been left hanging and that she had to be responsible.

But the other part of her said she'd be a wild idiot to miss out on spending quality time with him—in bed.

"Sounds good," she said.

He jogged around to hop in the driver's seat. She enjoyed riding around in his pickup with him. He waved to damn near everyone and drove in the easy, relaxed manner he did everything else in. No constant worry or speculation about his future and where he was going and if he was going to hit the next promotion milestone within his five-year plan. No tightness in his shoulders, no fretting over where to park or worrying about unwanted door dings and scrapes. Cash parked on the far end of the grocery lot where it was sparse, his big truck taking up two spaces.

They strode into the store next to each other and she was

peppering him with questions about how he liked his meat-loaf. A couple of girls passed them, giggling and greeting Cash. She glanced at him. His good humor didn't reach his eyes. He was being polite, that was all. After they were clear, his expression was pinched.

"It's okay, you know," she said.

"What's okay?"

"That a lot of girls *know* you."

He gave her tight smile. "It's one thing when it's in the past and forgotten. It's different when you're around someone and you care what they think about the past striding by all but announcing how we know each other."

Would now be a bad time to fist pump in the air? She wasn't like the others to him and he'd come close to admitting it. "Say I was your girlfriend; I wouldn't be jealous of your history. I'd be glad you settled down when you knew it was right and not when your family or society dictated it was. And I'd be even more pleased with it if you treated them right when you were with them."

His gaze darkened. "They were nothing but hookups. That's not treating anyone right."

She threaded her hand through his. Her girlfriend statement had opened a well of longing she didn't want to face alone. Being Ellis's girlfriend had taxed her mentally. A girl got tired of never being good enough, of always being judged. Being with Cash was the opposite.

She squeezed his hand as she steered him to the meat department. "If you had made a bunch of promises you had no intention of keeping, then I'd agree. Otherwise, it was you and another adult and a mutual agreement on a temporary transaction."

He chuckled. "That your fancy way of saying 'hookup'?"

"Yes. If your previous partners had grand ideas of a ring

and wedding dress, but you didn't lead them on, that's not your fault." She towed him to the hamburger display.

He shook his head, his mouth turned down. "Oh, honey. You're not asking a rancher to buy hamburger at the grocery store are you?"

"Umm…*I* was going to buy it."

"Nope." He led her away. An older man approached and stopped to chat with him.

Cash just introduced her by name, but didn't release her hand. He was a private man, not showy, but not hiding from others either. Her respect for him grew. The two men talked shop for a while, then they finished their trip.

With an armload of groceries, Cash loaded her and the bags up and drove back to his farm.

This was her vacation and she only had a week left. But she could get used to this every day of her life.

Abbi threw the pan in the oven and set it for an hour. She peered out the kitchen window toward the barn where she caught glimpses of Cash repairing the corrals that held his cows all winter. He was wearing his tan jacket and boots. His rugged jeans fit well enough to be catalogue ready, but as always, he wore a baseball cap. Was the hat his farmer side expressing itself? When Perry had talked about his ranching buddy, Reno, she'd expected a swaggering cowboy, much like Cash, only with a cowboy hat. In so many ways, he defied her expectations.

She grinned to herself and butterflies took flight in her stomach. Pushing away from the window, she looked around. What was she going to do for an hour that didn't include following Cash around like a lovesick puppy?

The inside of the house could use some TLC. It's not that

it wasn't cared for, it was just obvious he was a one-man show and everything outside the house was his priority. A light layer of dust lined the shelves, and the rugs could use a beating after the summer season, but she wasn't going to clean for him. One, it was her vacation and Ellis was probably enjoying her absence because he didn't have to chase her with a tidy list of atrocities she'd committed. And two, it was rude to be a guest in someone's home and clean like they weren't grown-ass adults who could do it themselves.

But boredom was setting in with fifty-five minutes to go.

She located her bag and withdrew her sketch pad. When she'd first arrived, she'd coveted the huge porch as a divine place to sit and sketch. Shrugging into a sweater, she figured out the time she had to draw before she had to finish supper and stepped outside.

An old porch swing creaked under her weight but felt sturdy enough. She curled one leg under herself and used her other foot on the ground to gently rock the swing.

The breeze sharpened with a chill now that the day was coming to an end, but Abbi wasn't rushing inside. She studied her surroundings. A long barn. Another big shed. Pastures dotted with cattle in the distance.

What should she draw?

A mew caught her attention. A gray and white tabby cat slinked toward her. The cat swiped itself along her leg. She giggled. A farm kitty, and a tame one at that. It'd been a huge challenge to catch cats at her grandparents' place, but Cash must give this little girl some lovin'.

The cat found a fading sun patch and curled into a ball like she owned the place.

It seemed Cash had a major soft spot for creatures. Abbi started drawing.

CHAPTER 12

Cash took his hands out of his work gloves and slapped the dirt off them against his leg.

His stomach growled. He was almost giddy at the thought of having a warm meal ready at the end of a long day.

But was he really looking forward to the food or the company?

This was the closest to a date he'd gotten since high school. She understood he meant to have sex with her yet she'd even cooked him dinner. She could've just as easily said she'd meet him later, or they could have gone out, but she seemed to like hanging out at his home.

He liked having her here. He'd never thought about being lonely, not with all his family around and stopping in anytime they wanted. But once Abbi left, he might just feel a little isolated and alone.

Nearing the house, he glanced up when he heard Alfalfa meow. His number one mouser arched her back on the porch, then sauntered off.

Then Abbi's voice drifted to him and he spotted her on the porch swing.

"Really, cat? I'm almost done and you get up and walk away? Figures." She scowled at a notepad in her hands.

"She probably figures I rustled up some critters down by the barn and wants to go hunting." He loped up his porch steps.

Abbi half-heartedly glared at the cat. "Laugh's on her. She looks bald in my picture."

She flashed her drawing toward him and his brows popped up. "An artist, huh."

She flipped the cover over on the picture and tossed it beside her. "Not really."

He snatched it away before she could grab it and opened it back up. Sitting next her, he studied her drawing. They swung gently together.

Without knowing much about art, he'd still say she was talented. Maybe Alfalfa's individual pieces of fur weren't sketched in, but the kitty looked nowhere near bald. Abbi had captured the pure feline bliss of roasting in a sunbeam.

Instead of reassuring her that she didn't suck, he decided to show her. He found an empty page and held his hand out for her pencil.

She narrowed her gaze on him, but handed it over. He took a few minutes and did his best, but his scribbles wouldn't look out of place in an elementary school art fair.

"There," he said and gave it to her. "Out of the two of us, which one's an artist?"

Her mouth quirked and her eyes danced with appreciation. "To be fair, the cat wasn't modeling for you."

"Oh, Alfalfa models for me. Usually at five in the morning when she thinks I'm late with breakfast and decides to caterwaul outside the window."

She laughed and pushed out of the swing. "You make pussies sing."

"You bet I do." He followed her into the house. Warmth

and savory smells swamped him. "Do I have time to clean up?"

"Yep. It's done cooking, but I'll set the table and start yowling if you take too long."

He took off his boots and coat. "If you have the pipes that cat does, I'd be impressed."

"No. I can draw, I can't sing."

"Makes two of us."

He ran through the shower, keeping the heat down until it was nearly too cold to stand. He'd never needed much to be in the mood, but playful banter with Abbi was the biggest turn-on, one he'd never known he had. Hell, anything Abbi did seemed to send blood to his groin. Smile, laugh, cook, fall in the mud, didn't matter. He was primed for her.

For the first time, he wondered what her dating history was. Were they two peas in a pod, or was she the type to settle into a long, serious relationship? Another topic that didn't matter to him. As long as all the men were history. He wasn't his dad, but he certainly wasn't his mom and wouldn't tolerate a partner who stepped out and lied.

Was he thinking long-term with Daniels's sister? Maybe. Would Daniels have approved? Maybe not, but he'd only seen the young and dumb Reno.

He threw on clean clothes and found Abbi standing by the dining room table. She perused the pictures on the china cabinet he'd inherited from Gram. And by inherited, he meant that no one else wanted to pack up and lug the thing anywhere so it'd stayed with him.

She glanced at him over her shoulder; her gaze heated. He wore his church outfit—black jeans and a striped button-up shirt—even nicer than what he went to the bar in.

"You guys all look alike. How many cousins total?"

He pulled out a chair for her to sit in. "Ten. Dillon and Brock are only children. There's me and Sissy.

Aaron has two younger brothers. One's still in high school and one's in middle school. And Travis has one brother and a sister. He's Sissy's age, and she's a couple years younger than Travis and travels the world for work."

She sat down and started dishing up their meal. He held back a grin at getting waited on. It seemed like if he cooked, he served her and if she cooked, she served him.

"Must've been fun growing up, having all those cousins around," she said.

"Still is. We get together all the time, but not everyone can make it anymore."

They dug into their food and fell into easy chatter. He talked about his family and she described summers at her grandparents'.

She placed her silverware on her plate and pushed her hair out of her face as she eyed the dish with the meatloaf, potatoes, and carrots. "We can throw the whole thing in the fridge. I already did the dishes, so it's just the plates for cleanup."

He sat back. His stomach was full and content, his taste buds were alive with the best dinner he'd had in a long time, and his only concern was relieving the steady pressure that had built since the previous night when he'd held her in his arms.

"The dishes can wait."

She nodded, glanced at him and paused. His expression must clearly state what was on his mind. Could she read in his eyes that he wanted to strip off that adorable college sweater of hers and lick every creamy inch of skin?

She pushed away from the table and sauntered toward him. Leaning down to his ear, she whispered, "And just what should we do all night?"

He snaked his arms around her waist and dragged her

onto his lap. "I'm going to help you remember what we did together the first night we met."

Her pupils dilated. She wiggled on his lap, a motion that felt too good. She draped her arms around his neck; he finally had her where he wanted her. He pressed his lips to hers.

She tasted of dinner and the Abbi he'd become addicted to. Her unique flavor of life and woman, mixed with the seasoning of her excellent meatloaf. His rancher's heart was securely roped.

Before his erection grew too uncomfortable, he hugged her to him and stood. She released his mouth to gasp at the sudden movement, but he only smirked. She held on while he carried her to his bedroom. Briefly, he'd thought of veering off into the guest room that she'd slept in, but having her in his bed was more temptation than he could refuse.

Inside, he set her down and lifted her sweater over her head.

"Do you remember when I first stripped you down?" He tossed the top to the floor. Her breasts filled out her pink lacy bra. He considered leaving it on. But no, it'd have to be replaced with his hands and mouth.

Her breath hitched and her hands landed on the clasp to her pants. "No. Yes. I remember being really excited."

The corner of his mouth hitched up. "Excited is a good start. What do you feel now?"

"Needy," she panted.

Oh yes. Him, too. He placed his hands over hers and undid her pants. Then he squatted to slowly drag them down, flaring his hands over her satiny skin. Her body rippled under his touch and he glanced up at her. Her luminous gaze stayed on him, but she stood still.

She stepped out of her pants. When she was back on both

feet, he pressed a kiss to her belly. A soft puff of air escaped her.

"You did the same thing before." He licked a path to one hip and nipped it, causing her to flinch and moan. He straightened and she tipped her head back to meet his gaze.

She lifted her hands to undo his buttons, but he grasped them in his. "Let me," he murmured. "I remember when I stripped you naked. You were spread out on the bed like a feast for the eyes. I want to feast again, Abbi."

Her pink tongue darted out to lick her bottom lip. "Yes."

Yes. He could relive that night together for a long time and it'd never decrease his satisfaction. That night had blown his mind. Reaching behind her, he unhooked her bra and slid it down her arms. Her breasts were freed. The bra landed on the sweater.

It was his turn to lick his lips. He wanted a taste, but he'd wait until she was laid out before him.

Next off was her panties.

Finally. She was naked. In his house. In his bedroom. She crawled onto the bed and flipped to her back. Just what he'd asked for. She'd presented herself for him.

He loosened the top button of his shirt. "I remember what you tasted like. It's kept me up at night since then. I want it again."

Prowling up the bed until he loomed over her, he hesitated for a moment. What if this was making her uncomfortable? What if she started to feel like he'd taken advantage of her?

She cupped his face. "I woke up with a raw throat from crying out. I want that again."

His worries washed away. It was one thing for him to yearn for another night with her, but to hear the same level of need in her voice was deeply gratifying. "You were a noisy one. I liked it." He dropped a brief kiss to her lips. "You won't forget my name after tonight."

He settled his weight between her legs and trailed a path of kisses down her neck. He drew one nipple into his mouth, then quickly moved on to the other. Her satiny center called to him and he didn't want to linger too long before he made her yell his name.

She squirmed under him, the heat from her core driving his own desire crazy. His cock pressed against his pants. He relished the discomfort, it kept him from rushing their time together. Soon he'd have her. But first...

Hitching her knees up and to the side, he noticed her fisting the covers of his bed. When he gauged her expression, he found desire, near desperation. He dipped his head down, found her clit. She rocked up.

She was as hot as he remembered, already wet for him. He'd probably stain his pants making himself wait before he finally sated himself with her body. But just like before, once wasn't going to be enough.

She sucked in a breath and moaned, almost drawing too far away from him. He tugged her closer to lick a path from her swollen clit to her opening. When he speared her with his tongue, she bucked almost off the bed. He wanted to grin, but instead, circled the swollen nub, her body shaking with the impending release.

He rose to his knees, increasing the pressure.

"Cash!" Her knees rose higher as she tensed every muscle in her body.

He raised his gaze. She watched him. Her eyes bright, her mouth open with shallow breaths. The sight of him between her legs must be heightening her pleasure. Her body spread before him certainly did it for him.

Suddenly her body spasmed. She threw her head back, calling his name. He inserted a finger. She jerked again as her sex clamped around his digit. His name left her lips in another cry. Her body shook and shuddered until she went limp and he eased up. This was how he wanted her—completely his.

He rose to his knees and, one at a time, undid the buttons of his shirt. "Did that bring back any memories, honey?"

Did it ever. She'd remembered snippets of their night together, but he was meticulously stitching them into one cohesive memory. Although his room was way better than the dive of a motel they'd been in.

She'd just had a record-breaking climax, but the sight of him shrugging out of his shirt primed her for more. A dull throb settled in between her legs, not allowing her to fully descend from the peak.

He tossed his shirt, and muscles rippled along his torso as his biceps flexed. Her mouth watered. Would he let her have her way with him? Her gut said not for a while. He was seriously re-creating their first night together.

Down went his zipper and she strained to see his shaft, remembering the length had been impressive. His cock sprang free.

Oh yeah. His erection twitched under her attention.

She bit her lip and caught his eye. "At what point did I suck on you?"

Fire flared in his gaze. "Right after I rode you hard." A slow, sexy grin spread along his face. "I have to admit, in case you don't recall, the first time went kind of fast. You had me all worked up."

"Mmm." She reclined. He shoved his pants down to keep them out of the way. "Now, how did I do that when I've barely touched you?"

His gaze swept her body. "If you could see what I see, honey…"

Honey was so generic, but he made it sound like he used it just for her. He snagged a condom from his pocket and rolled it on. One down. She was almost giddy. If he was truly giving her a repeat, they had two more condoms to go through.

He settled over her, forearms on either side of her head. His shaft pressed against her entrance. She tightened her legs around him.

"God, Abbi." He thrust in with a groan and didn't stop. "What'd I say. You got me worked up."

She twined her arms around him and smashed her mouth to his. He set a rapid pace, just like before, and took her hard. Her body was still sensitized from her climax and she was going to hit another peak. She crested like a rollercoaster car and careened into a void of pure ecstasy. There was nothing but her and him and how he made her body feel, and it'd be nothing if he didn't also make her feel like an extraordinary woman.

She moaned and hollered. He was right. She was noisy. A new trend—she'd never been one to shout before. But her world had never been rocked as hard as this, either. Everything with Cash was so much more, from something as simple as cooking a meal to eardrum-shattering sex.

He tightened, his thrusts shortened, and he grunted out his release while holding her close. Their connection was solid; they finished together. Then he collapsed on top of her, his body making little jerks as his orgasm faded.

She laid little kisses along his jaw and roamed her hands up and down his broad back. "You need to take those pants off because I want a good look at you naked."

He chuckled softly into her neck, still boneless.

She rolled them onto their sides, but he didn't stay,

getting up to shuck his pants. Before he tossed them, he grabbed another condom and put it on the bed. He rid himself of the first condom and laid back down next to her, snagging the second packet in his fingers.

He was about to rip it open, but she stayed his hand.

"Is this where I get to…?"

"Oh yeah."

"Then leave that off this time."

He paused and glanced up, his expression cautiously hopeful. "Are you sure?"

"It's all right, right?"

Ugh. The STD talk never got less awkward.

He nodded, but still looked like he didn't want to believe she was willing. "It's a small town. If someone's having problems, word gets around and…" He shrugged. "I've always used protection. Always."

"All right then, cowboy, on your back." She rolled up to her knees and straddled him.

"I go by rancher, or farmer. Not cowboy. The difference is in the hat."

She fisted his length, fighting her giggles. When had sex been so *fun*? She was comfortable with him, not doubting herself or just seeking release. She was enjoying this on so many levels.

Taking him into her mouth, she swirled her tongue up and down, tasting his salty spend from earlier. She moaned over him; he rolled his hips up in response. His hands landed in her hair. With her ass in the air, she worked up and down an erection that was as solid as the first time.

"I couldn't forget this." His hands tightened. "The way you sucked and licked. Abbi, you— Oh—" He gently lifted her away. "I need to come, but this is the point where you crawled on top of me."

She snagged the condom and ripped it open. Next time,

she was going to finish him. But it seemed important to Cash that they recreate their first night together. And she wanted it, too.

She recalled climbing his body and ever so slowly sinking down on to him. So she did. Her head dropped back and greedily accepted the pleasure that part of him gave her. He cupped her breasts in his hands.

"Now, if you remember," he drawled, "I lay back and you did all the work." His thumbs strummed her nipples. She shivered and curved herself into his hands.

"Good try. I clearly recollect how you latched onto my hips and set the pace."

His eyes hooded, he skimmed his hands down just as she'd described. "Because I loved the way your breasts bounced."

And they did. He curled up to her. She hugged him closer and he set another pace, this one less frantic. Her breasts bounced against his chest and their tongues danced. She made needy little moans and whimpers that would have been embarrassing, but he was making her body feel too good.

He broke their kiss to sear a path with his lips to her ear.

"You make me so fucking hot, honey."

Her sex quaked at the deep hunger in his voice. *She* did that. This wasn't a one-way street where he held all the power. She drove him just as crazy as he made her.

"The way you clench around me, like you can't get enough." He nipped at her earlobe. "Drives a man crazy."

She was almost at the precipice, almost ready to bowl over as he stroked her center, but then he wedged a thumb between them and circled her clit. He'd barely made it one complete round before she broke apart.

"Oh— Yes, Cash!" She rode him harder from this angle, her needy sex trying to get as much of him as possible.

"That's it, honey, fall apart in my arms."

She cried out his name again and squeezed her eyes shut. She saw stars behind her lids, heard him yelling his orgasm, shuddering inside of her.

Perfect.

Could this get any better?

Yes. Because she remembered a third condom.

He gently twisted them to the side. His shaft slid out and they lay together, letting their breathing even out. He floated his fingers down her arm and over her torso, teasing around her breasts and hips. They were both satiated, but he didn't seem to want to stop touching her. Her belly warmed and she snuggled into him.

"Your skin is so soft." His kissed her nape.

"Your body is so hot—in many ways."

Hot breath tickled over her skin. "Glad you think so."

"Me and half the county probably," she joked. "No one can deny how good you look."

"I like that you like it, though."

She blinked at his honest tone, like he didn't care what anyone thought of him but her.

This guy could be hard to walk away from. Lying in his arms, she had a hard time remembering why she should go back to Green Bay.

And that spurred a flashback. She'd thought the same thing that first night, when they'd lain like this, idly chatting. Even then, going home had seemed a dismal prospect.

But she wasn't packing her things and settling down in Moore after knowing Cash for a week. It wouldn't be feasible, and she needed time to consider that momentous of a change.

She patted his hand and rolled out from under him. "I need to go clean up."

He watched her go, and she wasn't self-conscious at all that she didn't wear a strip of clothing. But when she entered the bathroom, he was right behind her. He was holding up a third foil packet. Suddenly, an image bombarded her of watching them in the mirror as he entered her from behind and took her for a third time. She'd gasped and pleaded that he bring her to another climax and he had, but he'd teased and taunted. The edge had been taken off and he'd had all the time in the world to play with her body until she'd been nearly out of her mind.

She couldn't help her grin as she gripped the counter and wiggled her bottom. "Now this, I remember."

ash's eyelids opened and he frowned at the ceiling. It was lighter out than when he normally woke. A soft sigh next to him reminded him why he'd slept later than normal.

That third time. She'd been wanton. Issuing demands and making all kinds of noises that would've been his undoing if they hadn't had sex twice before.

Three times in one night was pretty damn admirable, and he'd only been able to do that twice now—both times with Abbi.

Carefully disengaging from her, he got out of bed and dressed in his work clothes. If she was still asleep when he was done with chores, maybe he'd make her breakfast.

He walked out to the kitchen and frowned at a vibrating noise. He scanned the room and found it was coming from her bag. Were her parents trying to get ahold of her? Should he wake her up and let her know she'd missed a call?

He shrugged it off; he'd tell her when she woke up.

The morning was quiet compared to yesterday, when he'd had fun, sexy company for his chores. She'd had such a good time, genuinely excited about what he did for a living. She was here for one more week. How would she like to help move cattle? As long as she could stay on a horse, or stand and wave her arms around to keep cattle from veering off, she'd be okay.

Yeah, he'd asked her to join them. His cousins wouldn't mind. They might start asking questions he wasn't sure how to answer, ones he'd have to talk with Abbi about, eventually. What happened after she went home? He couldn't imagine going back to his routine of heading to the bar for a quick hookup. But then, he wasn't desperate and he could just hang out at home and either work on the house or Netflix and chill. With the cat. Because that wouldn't be lonely at all.

He shook his head as he worked the controls to unload the hay bale into the feeder. No, he refused to be scared of his own company. Is that what had kept Mom around so long, so afraid to be by herself that she'd rather raise her husband's baby from another woman? Or had she been so blindly in love with Dad that she'd been willing to tolerate the affairs? It'd taken several years before Sissy had come along, and while Mom had never discussed fertility struggles, maybe that had had something to do with it.

Fuck, he didn't know. All he knew was that he didn't want to be like either parent when it came to relationships. Which was one reason why he resolved, as of now, to quit the bar scene even if Abbi left his ass in the dust.

The cattle were fed, and he idled the tractor back. The sun was coming out. He inhaled deep. Had he just decided to commit to a woman?

Yeah. He had.

But then there was her brother. Could he keep from revealing the depth of her brother's despair? She couldn't find out. As a brother himself, Cash reckoned that it's not what Daniels would've wanted. Cash wouldn't want Sissy to despair over his own personal pain. Hell, he'd protected Sissy from almost everything, just like Daniels probably had with Abbi. No. No way could she learn how depressed her brother had been.

He parked the tractor, tended to the horses, and fed the cats. Alfalfa was the friendliest one. A couple of the others flat-out ignored him, but he didn't mind as long as they kept mousing.

In case Abbi was still sleeping, he quietly entered the house.

Her words drifted to him from the kitchen. "I'll come home when my vacation's done. But things have changed and that's just the way it is." She paused. "No, it's not impulsive. People change." Something hard slapped the counter. "No, it's nothing like that. Geez, Mom, why is it always—"

He came around the corner. She had her back to him with her head hanging.

"I'm sorry, Mom, but— No. I've tried talking to him, he doesn't understand." Pause. "No, I *do* understand and I'm serious."

Cash knocked lightly on the doorframe. Abbi spun around, her brows lifted in surprise, one hand twisting in her hair, the other clenched around the phone. She untangled her hand and waved a greeting.

"It was nice talking to you, Mom." Abbi held his gaze and shook her head that no, it wasn't a nice talk. "Just try to trust me. I'm doing fine. Better than fine. This was a good decision. Love you, bye." She clicked off and muttered, "I'm a grown woman."

"Nice visit?" He crossed to her and kissed her forehead. She leaned into him, resting her head on his shoulder.

"How can they make me feel like I'm ten years old?"

"What are they so worried about? Have you never gone off and done something on your own?" Nuzzling her hair, it dawned on him that he didn't know much about her personal life.

"To be fair, I don't have the best track record of decision-making on my own. And I haven't done anything like this, by myself or with anyone."

He set her away from him and pinned her with a hard stare. "Be honest. Who's judged your decisions in the past? And did they use their standards or yours?"

She scrunched her nose. It was adorable. He was toast. "Well…I tend to follow my gut, not consider the consequences."

"Do you deal with the consequences?"

"Yes. I guess. But I haven't caused any major upsets. Just a lot of little ones that made my parents worry."

"News flash, honey. Parents are going to worry no matter what."

She rewarded him with a small smile. "Brothers, too?"

"We're a lost cause. Hungry?" He might be okay with his decision to keep the darkness of Daniels's last days to himself, but he didn't want to encourage any questions.

She nodded and slumped at the little dining set in the kitchen. "I didn't get a chance to eat. They kept calling until I answered."

Her parents were tenacious. He rummaged through the fridge and popped out with eggs and bacon.

"I suppose they'd freak if you told them about us."

She contemplated him, her gaze solemn. "Yes, they would. It'd be more proof of how I don't think through things." She waited a heartbeat, twisting her hands in her lap. "What about us, though? Is this more than…"

He set everything on the counter and faced her. Good, they were having this talk. "Yes, Abbi. You're more than. Don't doubt it. I'd like to see where this goes."

She tilted her head, her expression introspective. Then a

smile spread across her and she glanced down at her hands. "I'd like that, too."

Happiness shined brighter in him than the sun outside. "Good. I'd also like to see where we go right after we eat." He winked and dug out a bowl to start cracking eggs.

"I dunno," she said with a sly, sexy tone that went straight to his cock. "You have a lot of land. We could go a lot of places."

He cooked in record time and they wolfed down their food. She left the table, put her plate on the counter, and sauntered backward out of the kitchen.

"I'll do the dishes if you can catch me in ten seconds. One —" She darted out the front door.

Oh, he'd catch her no matter what, and the dishes wouldn't matter when he did.

He tore out of the house and raced in the direction of her laughter. She jogged around the house into the backyard. When she saw him give chase, she squealed and tried to speed up.

But it was too late. He tackled her, more an impromptu dance than anything violent. He wrapped his arms around her and lowered them both to the cold ground, twisting to keep her on top of him. Even his ball cap stayed on.

"That was a smooth move," she said breathlessly. Her hair hung between them, her arms coming around his neck. "Do it often?"

"To unruly calves that don't want me to take a look at them." His grin was lopsided because damn, this was *fun*. He hadn't realized how boring his days could be. Her bottom ground down over his hardening length and he rolled up into her. "I don't know what you're planning, honey, but I don't have any protection on me, and if you keep doing that…"

She wiggled delightfully as she reached into her jeans' pocket. "Just so happens, I snuck one from your stash."

He snaked a hand around her neck. "The rest is up to you. It won't be my ass hanging out in the wind."

"I trust you'll keep me warm." She pushed off him, then rose to her knees and straddled him while undoing her pants. Once she'd wrestled one leg out of her pants and underwear, her sex was bared to him. All blood rushed to his groin. He couldn't free himself quickly enough. He tried to cup her mound, but her need must have been raging as hard as his. She batted his hand out of the way and rolled the condom over his length, her cool hands an erotic contrast to the heat running rampant between them.

With no preamble, no more foreplay than a quick chase, she rose and settled herself over him. He gripped her waist but didn't move her until she was ready. She bit her lip and moaned. His gaze shot back down to where they were connected. In the bright light of day, she was even more sexy and gorgeous and brilliantly unhinged, and there were no shadows to hide it.

The grass crunched under him, not completely brown yet for the autumn season. He would worry about her catching a chill, or getting grass strains on her knees, but the whimpers coming from her sounded like nothing but pleasure. She rode him, her enjoyment of his body obvious, and he was soon swept up in sensation, raising his knees to tip her forward and thrust deeper. She arched into him and he gathered her to him, stealing her lips for a greedy kiss. They hadn't even done that before he'd entered her.

This girl was phenomenal. Her rhythm increased. He tried to match, tried to distance his mind so he didn't explode before her. Sweeping his tongue into her mouth, he savored the extra contact. It made him even more possessive. He hugged her tighter and thrust harder. They groaned and panted into each other until she briefly tensed, then bucked her hips. She tried to cry out, but Cash swallowed the sound. His peak slammed into him; his embrace tightened and he spilled his release.

They finally broke apart, gazing into each other's eyes. Could she feel it, too? This time was different. It wasn't mad hookup sex. It wasn't recreating an event to make sure she'd never forget their night together. This time had been about them. A promise that they had a future.

She stroked his face. He could get addicted to the tender light in her eye.

A truck engine made both their heads spin toward the road.

"Perfect fucking timing, Dillon," Cash growled. He eased Abbi off him and helped her back into her bottoms. They were in the middle of his yard; the trees should block the worst of what they'd been doing.

"Do you think he saw?" she hissed, pink staining her cheeks. From the orgasm or because she was ready to die of embarrassment? "I'm sorry."

"I'm not sorry about anything we did." He helped her up and brushed dried grass off her clothes. He rubbed her back and led her around to the front door. He didn't want this experience to make her skittish about hooking up anytime, anywhere. He wanted to make sure she was comfortable having sex in the backyard, the barn, the pastures, his truck —wherever the hell she wanted it. He was onboard.

"I just shouldn't have—"

He bent down and nipped her neck. She squeaked, giving him a playful swat. He chuckled. "You should've, and I can't wait until you do it again. Like you said, I've got a lot of land."

Finding her hand, he wrapped it in his. She gave him a grateful look. Was it the talk with her parents that had her second-guessing her actions? Or was she that flustered that Dillon might've seen them together? She could've walked buck naked down the road and Dillon wouldn't care. He was dopey over Elle. Cash, on the other hand, might get a lecture about getting close to Daniels's sister when she'd come looking for closure.

Well, he might not be able to give her closure, but he could love her.

Cash swallowed. Where the hell had that thought come from? He was just thinking of having his first adult relationship. But, no, it made sense. He wasn't about to get serious with someone he couldn't love.

Abbi squeezed his hand. They rounded the house just as Dillon was getting out of his pickup.

Dillon's brows rose when he spotted Abbi and his smile faltered. "Hey. I was just checking to see if you wanted help fixing fence since we're moving cattle next week."

Cash bristled at Dillon's tone. Only last spring, they'd mended their own figurative fences after Dillon had spent a couple years resenting Cash for being an unreliable prick. And while Cash might've fooled around with women, he'd never brushed off work.

"Yeah, I was just heading out there." He might've detoured into the bedroom to feast on Abbi for another hour, but hopefully she'd still be here when he was done. He tugged Abbi under his arm. "Dillon, I told you about Daniels's sister, Abbi."

Abbi hooked an arm around Cash's back, her grip tight, like she was anchoring herself to him. Was she nervous to talk to Dillon?

Her smile was hesitant. "I came to Moore to find you two and learn more about him."

Dillon's gaze softened. "I'm sorry about his death, Abbi. I

wish…I wish I could've done more. I've never felt so paralyzed in my life."

She shook her head. "I know it wasn't your fault. I'm sorry, I didn't come here to break open old wounds." She shuffled her feet and pressed closer to Cash. "I just wanted to know about his last day. He was here one day and the next he was—" She cut off with a choking sound.

Cash squeezed her shoulder and kissed the top of her head, a move that earned him a hard look from Dillon. Cash countered it with his own challenging glare.

"I can try to answer any questions," Dillon said. "But I doubt I have much more to tell you than Cash has." He shot Cash a look that said, *Have you even told her anything?*

Cash rolled his eyes as if to say, *Of course, I've talked to her but I haven't told her that.*

Abbi drew in a stilted breath. "You know what, I think I'm okay. Cash has told me some stories about Perry and I really don't want to make you two relive that horrible day."

Dillon ducked his head. "Daniels was a good soldier." Cash nodded, too, because he had been until his last few days. "But feel free to talk anytime. Cash can give you my number."

"Thanks. I appreciate it. I can see why he talked about you two all the time. Said both of you should buy a lotto ticket for getting stationed together."

It'd definitely been unusual, but Cash wouldn't have survived the eight miserable years without Dillon, even if they weren't stationed together they still coordinated their leave. At the time, he'd told himself he was staying in the army for Dillon, but it had really been because he hadn't wanted to come back home and be the mediator between his parents again. And it made him feel like utter horseshit that the only reason his parents had moved away and left him the house was because Dillon's dad had gotten sick and passed away, showing them life was too short to be miserable together. All his uncles must've been going through some shit because they'd agreed to sell the farm and ranch operation to Cash and his cousins.

"You gonna be okay here while Dillon and I head out? Make yourself at home and—" he dug his keys out of his pocket, "—take the truck if you need to run any errands."

Abbi peeled away, letting go of his hand last. "Nice to finally meet you, Dillon. You boys have fun."

Cash watched her sway into the house and gave her a final wave. Dillon watched him.

"I don't fucking believe it," his cousin muttered.

Cash snapped his gaze back. "What?"

Dillon shook his head. "I saw you two and thought you were stalling and bluffing and using her until she lost interest and went back home. But you really like her."

Cash glanced at the house again. Abbi was inside "making herself at home" and the rightness of it settled deep into his bones. "Yeah. I do. Mom wasn't thrilled." He winced. What had made him confess that?

"Aunt Patty's not the one dating her. Look, I know—"

Cash arched a brow for him to finish, but Dillon grimaced like he'd swallowed pickle juice.

"I know," Dillon continued, "your parents have had shit going on and it's more than affected you. But I don't want to see you in forced isolation because of their drama."

"I *am* their drama."

"No." Dillon vehemently shook his head. "You're their child. Whatever happened was between the two of them, but even I could see you took the brunt of it."

Cash took his hat off and swiped his hand through his hair before putting it back on. "I told them about meeting Frankie every week."

"Good."

"I'd like to invite her out, you know, sometimes—for meals and shit."

"Good. She's your grandma, too."

"It's just…when I think about the shit I went through, I think of her. She lost her daughter and her grandson for almost twenty years. She just has two fat cats for company."

Dillon clapped him on the shoulder. "Not anymore."

Cash sucked in a deep breath and shook all the emotion off. "Let's grab our tools and I'll tell you about Sissy's new escapade."

CHAPTER 14

*A*bbi stepped back to eye her handiwork. She worried her bottom lip. Would he be upset? Had she been too presumptuous when she'd found the gallon of paint and all the painting supplies in the closet of the guest room?

To be fair, he'd told her to make herself at home and a girl could only sketch so much. She studied the warm earth tone she'd painted on the walls. Whoever had chosen this color of taupe had a good eye. The woodwork came alive under something other than dingy white and before she'd started, she inspected the room. Someone had peeled off wallpaper.

The paint had almost begged her to slap it on.

Her hair was pulled back in a ponytail and she was stripped down to her undershirt, wearing a borrowed pair of what she hoped were old basketball shorts. Flecks of paint dotted her top and the shorts and she probably had a few smears on her face.

The oven beeped. She bounced out of the room to take the roast out. Whenever she thought of returning home, it cast a gray cloud over her day. This was nice. Wake up to breakfast cooked by a hot man, have some sex, putter around and paint, and fix supper out of whatever was around. Her creative juices were flowing and, god, she'd missed that.

She hadn't even missed not having access to her phone. She'd shut it off since she'd already talked to Mom, and Ellis wouldn't quit calling. She'd even texted him to stop and he'd said if she picked up he would. That's when the power button had gotten hit.

For hours, she'd been lost in painting, had found a long lost part of herself. It wasn't that she regretted what she'd gone to school for. It'd been a good, solid decision—her own decision. But she mourned having let her hobbies fall to the wayside while she'd dealt with life in the wrong ways. Instead of depending on Ellis, she should've whipped out her colored pencils until she figured it all out.

She heard men's voices outside the window. She peeked out. Dillon was driving off and Cash was swaggering up the walk. So damn sexy. And he was all dirty and sweaty, probably skipped lunch. She bit her lip. Hopefully, he wouldn't freak when he saw she'd painted without asking.

The front door opened. "Honey, I'm home."

She probably glowed with those words as she went out to meet him.

He sniffed. "Did you cook? Lord, that smells delicious."

"I figured I owed you two meals since technically you're providing the food."

He waved it off like it was no big deal and she believed him, had started to crave his easygoing nature.

"Um…but first can I show you something?"

He nodded but eyed her outfit, like he couldn't place why she'd be streaked in paint.

She led him to the guest room. He whistled and took his hat off. The way his hair was crushed down from being in a hat so long was adorable.

"I hope it's okay." She crossed her arms and held her

breath. If she got berated about having to ask first and plan, she'd understand. It wasn't her house.

"You know how long that paint was sitting in the closet?" He wandered the room, looking around.

She shook her head, unable to read anything from his tone.

"Two years. I wasn't even sure it was good anymore."

She'd broken a sweat shaking it. "Do you mind that I went ahead and used it?"

"Of course I don't mind. But I don't expect you to work while you're here."

Her trepidation backed off and the tension drained out of her. "I want to. It was fun actually. Almost like one of those TV shows where I get to restore an old house."

He smiled down at her, his blue eyes twinkling. "Well, there's a lot of house here to restore. Go wild. I'm sure your taste is better than mine."

"Not if you're the one that picked out the color. It's perfect."

He chuckled. "It was Mom and Sissy's way of hinting that I needed to do something to the place." He grabbed her hand and led her out to the kitchen. "What's the reason for that glorious scent? Did you raid my meat again?"

A groan escaped when his eyes landed on the counter where she'd set the food to cool.

"You're amazing." He pulled her in for a quick kiss before retreating to the bathroom to wash his hands.

She served him a heaping plate and filled her own. They ate and chatted about their day. He talked of fences in the south pasture, by the north quarter, and other directions she didn't understand. Maybe they could go riding again so he could show her everything he was describing.

She picked up their plates. Normally, a touch of resentment haunted her when she cleaned the table, but that was because Ellis had "standards" that he expected to be maintained. Cash only directed her when she needed help finding where an item was stored. And as he put food into containers for the fridge, he seemed happy to help. She didn't even feel like he was helping her, but that they were in it together.

She got a rag damp and went to wipe the table. As soon as she leaned over it, he crowded behind her and nuzzled her neck.

"Do you mind if a dirty rancher has his dessert?"

She turned and gazed up at him. "As long as he doesn't mind if his dessert is just as dirty."

He didn't hesitate, pulling her close. They smashed their lips together, only breaking apart to get her shirt off. Her shorts came off next. He propped her on the tiny table and kissed a path to her sex. When his hot tongue hit her clit, she collapsed back onto her elbows.

Her orgasm hit faster than ever, but the sight of a rugged Cash between her legs would never fail to get her off.

Seconds after she'd crested, he rose and undid his pants to free himself. He was quickly stroking her to another climax. Something about this time was so much more intimate. Not just because they were having sex in his kitchen with the light on, but every stroke had the power of a hundred thrusts. It was like he was velvet-covered steel. The buttons of his shirt chafed her nipples in the most erotic way, but every nerve ending seemed more sensitized than usual.

She twined her ankles behind his back and when his hips jerked with his orgasm, she hit her second climax.

His hands pressed into the tabletop on each side of her as he growled her name. His hot release filled her and her eyes flew to his.

No condom.

They'd established they were safe. She didn't care, but would he?

Holding onto him while he drifted down from his orgasm, she peppered his face with kisses.

As he was withdrawing, his face went pale and his gaze flew to hers. "Oh shit. I forgot about protection." He glanced back down, an unreadable emotion flitting over his features. "I'm sorry."

Was he worried for her? "I'm on birth control. How do you feel about it?"

"Umm… It used to be my worst nightmare, but I…believe you about the birth control. Not that I don't ever want kids, just…" He seemed to struggle with what to say.

"I get it." With his history, she understood.

He gave her a lopsided smile. "That was amazing."

She snuggled into his strong embrace that kept her from collapsing back on the table. "I agree."

"I bet it'll feel just as good in the shower." He picked her up, her legs still wrapped around him.

He was right. It did.

Once they were dressed and had finished cleaning the kitchen, she stood in the doorway and shoved her hands in her pockets.

Cash leaned against the counter. "What do you want to do tonight?"

That was exactly what was on her mind. She knew what she wanted, she just had to broach the topic. "Would you mind running me into town so I can grab my stuff, maybe even…" Was she going to ask? What if he turned her down? After what they'd just shared, she didn't think so. "Maybe I could check out and stay here for a few days." *Until I have to go home and move out of my apartment.* Where would she go? Staying in Green Bay…well, it was her home. But the thought of leaving Moore left a big hole in her soul.

A slow, sexy smile spread across his face. "I guess you wasted a few nights of paying for a room."

"I wouldn't call them wasted." Though Ellis would've choked on his tie if he'd found out she had paid for a room she wasn't staying in. He'd probably think it was worse than staying with a man she'd met a week ago.

"I agree, but it's not my money." He crossed to her, his hands landing on her hips. "Let's go get you checked out."

They loaded into his truck. How easy it was between them. She'd wager Cash knew her better than anyone, even her parents. Oh, they knew her past and everything she'd done in life. But they had a mold they wanted her to fit into, and as long as she didn't buck the trend, they assumed they'd sculpted her how they'd wanted to.

On the way to town, her mind worked over her financials. She'd probably have to pay for the evening, but she'd planned for two weeks anyway. And she'd been eating off Cash's groceries, saving almost three nights' worth by just not eating out. Now she was saving on a hotel. The unintended benefit of meeting the man of her dreams was that she had some money left over for a deposit on her own place.

He hung an arm over the wheel as they cruised on the highway. "I'm going to talk to Sissy tomorrow. Tell her she needs to talk to Mom and Dad about her new career."

"You don't think she's said anything yet?"

He flashed her a look full of irony. "My phone's been quiet, so no."

"Shut it off. It's what I do."

He groaned. "Then they'd descend on me here. It's one thing when there's a family shindig, a whole 'nother when they're just here to complain to me."

He switched to more attentive driving and wove his way

through town, which took all of two minutes. Abbi stared out the window at the passing businesses that were closed for the night. Bars and gas stations were the only things open after eight at night in Moore.

"Wow. That dude looks pissed."

"Hmm?" Abbi glanced at him, then to where he was looking toward the hotel. She sucked in a breath, the blood draining from her face.

By her car in the parking lot was a familiar four-door sedan—a responsible ride, fuel efficient, and without a speck of dirt. Around the two cars stalked Ellis. Street lamps glinted off his plain brown hair, his suit jacket off and his tie loosened.

Her panic soon turned to seething anger. "Oh. My. God. He didn't."

His expression grew perplexed. "You know him?"

"Yes. And he's so dead."

"Who is he?" His tone was guarded.

Anger boiled through her veins. As soon as the pickup slowed to a stop, she jumped out. "Ellis, what the hell are you doing here?"

Cash got out, too, but hung back. She was grateful for his presence, refused to let Ellis cow her like he always had. Would someone else see how Ellis belittled her?

Ellis stopped where he was and clamped his hands on his hips. His expression was relief mixed with ire. "I'm here to help you."

"Why? We're over."

Ellis held his hands up. His typical placating stance. "Abigail. Couples in a committed relationship don't pull the plug during their first fight."

She sputtered. "First fight? What were the fights before that? You thinking I was being out of line for speaking my mind?"

"You two are in a relationship?" Cash's low voice carried through the angry words.

"Yes."

"No!" Abbi yelled. She stood in the headlights of Cash's truck. He hadn't moved away from his door.

Ellis drew himself up to his full height, still a couple inches shorter than Cash. He glanced at Abbi before settling his gaze on Cash. "Who are you?"

Her fury made her want to shriek and jump on Ellis like a feral cat. "*We* were supposed to come up here because this was important to me, but you decided it was *silly* and I was being *needy*. I'm so over how you treated me."

"And exactly how have I treated you? Who was with you when your brother died? Who got us our apartment?" Ellis gestured to her car. "What about the upgrade in wheels to a car that won't fall apart on the highway?"

She fisted her hands, fury freely flowing through her. He took credit for everything. "Last I checked, my paycheck paid for those things, too."

"Well, I'll leave you two." Cash stepped back into his pickup, his face carefully blank.

A lead weight sank through her insides. Oh *shit.* How did this look to him? "Cash, wait!"

He paused, his door almost closed.

From the pain in his eyes, she didn't have much time. She jogged to his window as she said, "Ellis and I aren't together anymore."

"Are you sure about that?" Cash tore his gaze away from her to an irate Ellis planted in front of his car. Cash switched his glare to out the windshield, his eyes shimmering with hurt and anger. "Sounds like you have some things to work through. Good thing you haven't checked out yet." He yanked the door shut and drove off.

With Cash's history, he had to be thinking all the wrong

things. She rounded on Ellis. He held up a hand again. She wanted to smack him.

"That," she stabbed her finger toward Cash's taillights, "is a man who respects me and treats me like a damn adult. Something I've been missing for the last three years."

Ellis's hand dropped. "Have you— Have you slept with him?"

"News flash!" He flinched, giving her a small spark of satisfaction. "None of your business. I was single when I got here and I regret nothing of what I've done since I've been here."

"Abigail…" Ellis sounded crestfallen. He swallowed and nodded. "I understand. Your brother's death was hard on everyone and you're still struggling. I…" A myriad of expressions ran across his face—pain, despair, determination. "You know what? It's my fault, too, but this is just a bump in the road. I'll try harder to understand now. Come on, let's go inside and talk."

She almost—almost—experienced a modicum of guilt over hurting him. But if he hadn't been so wrapped up in knowing what was best for her, they could've had this talk years ago. "I'm going inside to pack. Then I'm checking out." She wasn't going to squat in a hotel room with her ex and expect Cash to hear her out.

She palmed her key card and stormed into the hotel. Ellis trotted behind her to keep up.

"I'll help you carry your things, Abigail, and I can follow you back to Green Bay tonight."

Ellis thought she was checking out to go home with him?

Rounding on him, she kept her voice down to keep from disturbing guests and making a scene. "You don't understand. I'm not going anywhere with you. I'm checking out, then finding Cash to explain what just happened. You and I?" She waggled her finger between them. "We're done."

She resumed her mission. Four more doors until her room.

He was on her heels. "I understand perfectly. You're angry with me and you don't think clearly when you're emotional."

She fisted her hands but kept walking. The nerve of that man. It was always her, never him.

When she stopped in front of her room, he put a hand on the door. She turned her glare on him, but he kept talking. "I was wrong to stay behind and not come up here with you. I just…there was a thing at work, and being away for two weeks—my vacation time being used up for—"

Her irritation rose another notch. "And you blamed me instead of telling me how you really felt."

"I didn't see how important it was to you at the time."

She unlocked her door and slammed into the room. Silently, she gathered her toiletries, the clothing that had been hanging on the back of the chair. Ellis watched her. He was probably logging all the ways she'd been messy, storing the info away for future insinuations about how she wasn't as competent as he wanted her to be, or as her parents wanted.

"Who is he?" he said. His quiet, serious tone stalled her packing efforts.

If Ellis wanted to talk to her like an adult, she'd tell it to him straight. "Cash Walker. He's the guy who was with Perry when he died."

Ellis's throat worked before he got his words out. "You found him and then…then you two…"

She hadn't meant it to play out this way—not like this, with him thinking she was unfaithful, or so weak that she fell into the arms of the first man that walked by. And, well, that kind of had happened, but only because that man had been Cash. She would make a point about why she was with him.

"No, he found me actually, when I got to town. We talked

and one thing led to another. Then I found out he was the one they called Reno and we talked some more. For once, Ellis, I feel like someone understands me."

Ellis peered at her before his face screwed up. "You slept with him right after you met him?"

She growled in frustration. That was all he'd heard out of what she'd said.

"Yes," she snapped, banging her suitcase lid closed and zipping it. "And he's never held it over my head to get me to act like his puppet. I'm checking out, so if you're staying, you'll have to check into your own room. I have six more days of vacation. Don't worry about my belongings. I'll swing by and pack my stuff when I get home." *It'll be like I was never there.* How true was that? She hadn't painted even one wall in the place. The decor was all Ellis and anything of hers had been tucked away nice and neat. Their place together had no personality, just like her ex.

She yanked her luggage to the floor and rolled it with her as she strode out of the room with her head held high. That had felt good.

Cash nursed his beer and mindlessly flipped through channels until he found something that didn't remind him of Abbi or everything else in his life that made him feel like shit. It was impossible. He landed on the Hallmark channel and at the sight of the doe-eyed heroine gazing at her quirky love interest, he sped past. HGTV reminded him of Abbi's paint job and how nervous and proud she'd been. Football only brought back his fledgling years chasing girls and the echo of Mom's words in his head. He flipped to a music station and groaned when the lyrics about lost love registered. Why the fuck did he have cable in the first place?

He flipped the TV off and took another drink, barely tasting it. Looking around, he had to think hanging at the bar would've been better than sitting in his basement, down with a broken heart. He had thought the bar would've brought back memories of his first night conversing with Abbi. And then he might've gotten hit on and he had no interest in a quickie with someone who was, at the most, a casual friend.

He'd wanted to be alone with his heartache. Rubbing his chest, he grimaced. Was the beer giving him heartburn, or was this what it felt like getting betrayed? How had Mom done it? He and Abbi had grown close fast, but Mom had been *married*. Her hopes and dreams of a bright future had been dashed when Dad had dropped his zipper around the wrong chick.

And what the hell was wrong with Dad? How could he do that to someone he loved? Cash certainly couldn't love Abbi this soon after meeting her—he couldn't be that naive—but he had no wish to bed someone else.

But he and Abbi had only been together a week. A short week. Maybe Cash wasn't cut out for a relationship after all. If he'd buckled this quickly after all these years and then had picked a cheating girlfriend on top of it, maybe he was better off not changing his routine.

He polished off his beer and sank back into the couch. The floor above him creaked.

Dammit, was one of his cousins here? They were his best friends, but he didn't need anyone to witness the pathetic man he was turning out to be tonight.

"Cash?"

He almost dropped his beer. That was the last voice he'd expected to hear.

What the hell was Abbi doing here? And what a shitty night to forget to lock the door.

The floor creaked again and he jumped up. She'd find him

down here and he didn't need her getting that far into the house.

Taking the stairs three at the time, he was upstairs in seconds. She stood in his living room; her suitcase sat by the front door. When she turned toward his footsteps and her expression lit up, his chest tightened. All he wanted to do was grab her in his arms and claim her as his own, but he had his pride—and she had a boyfriend.

"What are you doing here?"

She exhaled and her shoulders dropped. "I checked out. I'm not staying with Ellis."

"Then get another room."

She stared at him for a couple of heartbeats. "I can imagine what it must've looked like to you, but I was a single woman when we met." She glanced around. "Can we discuss this?"

Yes, he wanted nothing more. "No."

Folding her arms across her chest, she pinned him with a hard stare. "I was a single woman when we met. I didn't tell you about him because I didn't feel the need to dwell on my past. The only reason I still have anything to do with him is because I have to move out of our apartment when vacation's over. Unless he's packed up my shit and taken it to my parents, which will be a scene to witness unto itself because they think he hung the moon and stars and that I'd be a lost little puppy without him."

Her voice was full of conviction, but Cash refused to buckle. She was single when they met, but she still lived with the guy? "Sounds like you two have some things to work out."

"No. We don't. He planned to come here with me, then backed out at the last minute. For some reason, thankfully, what he did finally tagged my last nerve. I couldn't take how he treated me anymore. I couldn't take how he and my parents ganged up on me and made me feel like a child over and over again. But after Perry died…" She crossed to the couch and sat down, her arm on the armrest, her forehead resting on her fist. "I didn't want to burden my parents with worrying about me since they lost a son and I'm all they have left. They approve of Ellis and he kept me within the limits of their approval, and that was enough for me. But, Cash, I was so fucking miserable. The night we met—yes, only hours after I'd become a single woman— was the first time I felt like me in a long time. And even then I was determined not to go back to being that girl because I knew breaking up with Ellis would hurt my parents. They'll be losing him, too. But I'm not going back to him."

The fence Cash was frantically trying to construct around his heart weakened. She sounded sincere. "Then why is he here?"

Frustration filled her eyes. "He's been trying to text and call. He acts like I threw a hissy fit and nothing more. That he just needs to talk some sense into me like always and I'll come back and be a good girl. When I told him about us, he called it a 'bump in the road.' What an ass. But at least it made him admit that he might've played a role in our breakup."

She seemed to wait for him to speak. She didn't fidget or nervously look around the room, but Cash wasn't a profiler or anything. His only reference point for this kind of situation was Mom crying and Dad stomping downstairs to sleep on the couch.

"What'd you tell him about us?" Why was that important? There was no them anymore. Was there?

"I was honest about how we met—I'm sure he'll hold it against me. I said that I feel like myself around you and I like how you treat me." Her small smile broke down even more of his figurative fences. Should've known the imaginary ones wouldn't last forever, just like the ones lining his property.

Fatigue weighed him down. It wasn't terribly late, but he'd been on an emotional rollercoaster for the last hour. He should kick her out but now that she was under his roof, he couldn't. Because he wanted to believe her even though all his learned instincts encouraged him not to. "Fine. Take the guest room. I'm going to bed." He pivoted to head down the hallway.

"Cash, I'm sorry. I had no idea he'd be so hard-headed about the breakup and I'm sorry it hurt you."

He slowed and pinched the bridge of his nose. Could he believe her? And if he did, did that make it better?

Slightly. Even single for hours was better than not single.

He let out a long exhale and trudged to his room. It was too much to deal with tonight.

CHAPTER 15

Cash woke up at his normal time, dressed quietly, and tiptoed out of his room. He felt like someone was going to jump out at him and yell "Coward!" They'd be right. He couldn't deal with Abbi after the raw night he'd had. The only thing he wanted to do this morning was feed his cattle and ride Patsy Cline. A couple hours on his horse tended to clear things up.

He made it outside and went for the tractor. If the engine woke Abbi up, he hoped she'd just give him time and not come and find him. Last night, he'd thought her proximity and honest-sounding words were the reasons he'd waffled and caved, to keep her around and see where their relationship went. But a night of restless sleep hadn't helped.

For years, he'd thought his number one fear was to be the cheating spouse his dad had been. Now, it was going through life miserable because he couldn't walk away from a bad thing in pretty packaging.

Problem was, he wasn't sure that was Abbi. He was afraid to believe her. Sure, his two minutes around Ellis hadn't made him a fan, but Cash didn't really know him, just had Abbi's claims.

The man had seemed arrogant, though. Not in the superficial sense, but intellectually. The way he'd looked at Abbi as if he'd been calming a petulant child had made Cash's blood simmer. He couldn't picture Abbi putting up with that. Had Ellis been the guy Daniels had worried about her trading her sense of self for?

Cash shook his head. Daniels had wanted to give Abbi financial freedom and all he'd likely done was drive her deeper into Ellis's control.

But depression probably didn't make a soldier think clearly when already thousands of miles away from home.

He wrapped up the feeding and parked the tractor. He half expected Abbi to come rushing out, but she didn't. He saddled Patsy Cline.

His horse nickered and turned into him. As he patted her neck and gave her a half hug, a smile pulled at his lips while he mentally defended his own actions. There was no shame in a man hugging his horse. She'd saved his sanity when he'd gotten out of the army. Cash had come home, reeling from his broken relationship with Dillon. He'd wanted to come back home so badly, for so many years, but had been dreading it just as much. And then Daniels.

The terror Cash had experienced when he'd lost his friend… He and Dillon had been through some shit before that with multiple deployments, but that had been the worst. Daniels had been the only one they'd lost. Dillon had blamed Cash because he'd known Cash was hiding something, but hadn't known Cash suspected that what Daniels had done was intentional.

If Cash had been more aware of what the other man had been going through mentally, maybe he could've helped

Daniels. Cash could've worked his way up the chain of command until someone listened to him. They could've made sure Daniels didn't go on any missions until his mental health was cleared. And there's the big what-if: What if he was wrong?

But he doubted it. Hindsight was crystal clear and full of regrets.

He rode Patsy Cline through the ditches at an easy pace. A couple of miles down the road, he spotted the gray outline of Dillon out for his morning run. He brought his horse to a trot to catch up. Dillon lifted his chin in acknowledgment. Cash steered her to the road and she kept up with Dillon, familiar with the routine. Sometimes Cash went for a run, too; sometimes he needed horse therapy instead.

"How far you going today?" Cash called.

"Five, just on my way back." Dillon slowed slightly to keep his pace conversational. "I thought you'd be rushing back to hang out with Abbi."

Cash dropped his gaze to his reins. "Yeah, about that."

Dillon didn't slow, but his gaze burned into him. "Did you fuck up or did she?"

The corner of Cash's mouth lifted. Dillon hadn't assumed it was all him and that said a lot about how far they both had come since they'd returned home. He explained what had happened. Dillon stayed quiet, keeping his easy pace. As the story poured out, some of the weight lifted from Cash's shoulders. Maybe it was the bright autumn day that made the situation not as black and white.

Cash finished and the only sounds were Dillon's steps and heavy breathing and Patsy Cline's hooves grinding into the gravel road.

"I guess it comes down to if you believe her or not," Dillon said. "Or if it matters."

"It matters. How could it not?"

"Because of your parents."

"Yep."

They fell quiet again. The entry to their driveways came into view. His on the left, Dillon's on the right. Dillon slowed to a walk and put his hands behind his head to cool down.

His cousin sighed and mopped his brow. "All I have to say is that I've never seen you like this. You took a chance on this girl, and I can't believe it was for nothing."

"To teach me a lesson about not taking chances on any more women."

"I don't mean to speak like some old wise bastard, but that's kind of what relationships are. Taking chances. Trusting. If you can't do that, then you either aren't ready for a relationship or she's not the right girl."

Cash's first instinct was to argue that Abbi was the right girl. He clamped his jaw shut and glared down the road. "I guess I can choose to believe her, and if it's not meant to be, it's not meant to be."

"How are you going to determine that?"

Cash shrugged and swung Patsy Cline toward his driveway. "I guess if she leaves my ass or something."

Dillon chuckled and then coughed from the exertion of his workout. "That's one way to look at it. Just don't expect to rush back in and be where you left off when what's-his-name arrived. It's not like starting over, but it kind of is."

"Listen to you, you wise old bastard."

Dillon flipped him off and strolled toward his own place, then stopped. "But it'll be better to be honest about Daniels earlier rather than later. He's been gone almost three years. It'll be hard for her, hard for her parents, but better in the long run." Dillon resumed his trek.

Better for who? Cash could sit on a secret like that and

not feel one ounce of guilt. Crashing Abbi and her parents' world was something he'd avoid. "I think it's best they don't know."

"I think so, too. But *you* know. And you're in a relationship with his sister, which also means his parents. Keeping it to yourself will only erode what's growing between you. But, hell, it's not like I can say do it or don't. It's a tough call." He tossed him a quick wave and continued back to his house.

No. There was no easy answer, no winners. Abbi's family had already lost. Cash's gaze landed on his house. Her car was in the driveway.

Dillon's first piece of advice registered. *Not like starting over, but it kind of is.*

Abbi scratched her nose with her pinky and the paintbrush she held swiped her hair. "Dammit!"

She squinted as she jerked it away from her head. Had she painted her damn hair?

Tossing the brush down on the tray, she scowled at the whole room. Painting today wasn't nearly as fun. Not even therapeutic. She'd had a crappy night's sleep, running through her mind what she should've done differently. A thousand scenarios and she really couldn't think of anything she could change. At no point had there been any reason to say, "Hey, I think my ex-boyfriend doesn't think he's my ex and while I technically still live with him, I refuse to spend one more hour under the same roof."

Maybe some of that should've come up?

Ugh. She snagged a rag off the ground and batted at her hair. Cash might be back soon, but did it matter what she looked like? He'd shut himself in his bedroom—without her

—and snuck off before she'd woken. But what had she expected, that everything would be back to the way it had been? For the thirtieth time she asked herself if she should just go back home. She'd done what had been dogging her and she'd faced Ellis. All that was left was moving out, and perhaps it was best to do that before she went back to work.

Then there were her parents. She'd purposely left her phone on silent, in her luggage.

Abbi stared forlornly at the paint tray. She had another wall to finish. If she completed the room and cleaned all her supplies up, would he even notice?

Would he notice if she just left?

The longer she pondered it, the smarter the idea sounded. She couldn't avoid her parents forever, and extra steel lined her spine after facing Ellis. Her parents couldn't bully her into getting back with him.

No, but they could berate her and constantly and comprehensively hound her about what she'd done until she caved on other issues just to make them happy.

God, she even knew she did it. It was like she regressed ten years around them. One mention of Perry and the conversation was over.

"Hey."

She whipped around. Cash leaned against the doorframe, his arms folded. His tan jacket couldn't hide his lean, muscular physique.

"Hey." Afraid to get her hopes up, she feathered her hair away from her head.

His gaze drifted to her paint-splattered hair. He didn't exactly smile, but the heaviness in his gaze lifted just a little. "You don't have to paint."

"I didn't want to leave." Her honesty surprised even her. She forced herself not to fidget under his vivid blue gaze.

"I'm glad you didn't," he finally said.

Relief swelled, but she tamped that shit down. He had hang-ups for a good reason. This was new territory for him. Her, too.

"You are?" she asked. Yeah, they were making leaps and bounds in this relationship, but it was more than she'd expected when she'd woken up to an empty house.

He adjusted his baseball cap and recrossed his arms. "You were kind of right. Ellis is none of my business and you said you were single when we met. I either believe you or I don't." His serious expression didn't bolster her hopes that he truly believed her, or wanted to. "I'd like to trust you."

"I choose to trust you."

His brows popped up. Had he not thought it took trust on her part, too?

She lifted a shoulder in a shrug. "When I go back to Green Bay, I have to know that you're not trolling town for women, just like you have to trust that I'm not—" she wrinkled her nose in distaste, "—dabbling in life with Ellis."

"The only pussy I plan to pick up is Alfalfa. And maybe Dutchie and Baron. Oh, and Dillon has Trixie and Dixie."

A smile tugged at her lips. "That's getting to be a lot of pussy."

He grinned. "What can I say? They can't resist me." He pushed off the door and crossed to her. He gently picked at the paint in her hair. "Hungry?"

In so many ways, but she sensed it was too soon for intimacy, though the conversation they'd just had was deeper than any she'd had in previous relationships.

"I didn't eat breakfast."

Regret flashed through his gaze. He dropped a kiss on her forehead. She shut her eyes and let his heat soothe her raw nerves.

"Brunch it is." When he left the room, she immediately wanted him back.

She'd almost lost him, and it had disturbed her. Before Ellis, her long-term relationships had been shallow. With Ellis, it'd been one-sided, with her giving him all the power. But she and Cash were on equal footing, like partners should be.

She cleaned up her paint supplies. Cash's voice drifted in; he must be on the phone.

Wandering through the rooms, she mentally tallied what she'd need if Cash gave her free rein to dress them all up. Only she couldn't stop at paint colors. Window dressings danced across her mind and she ran a finger along the trim. It could use a good overhaul, too. Her creative side luxuriated in the possibilities. To go from paper to an actual, real-life canvas was heaven. At home, she'd always helped Mom and Dad, but decor had been their decision. Abbi and Perry had followed their commands.

Finishing her daydreams in the living room, she stayed out of the kitchen. From his even tone, Cash must be talking to his family. What was he saving them from now?

No wonder he and Perry had gotten along. She'd told herself she was coming here for closure, for answers even, but she hadn't known about what. She'd overheard Mom often crying to Dad. Why had it just been Perry killed? Of course, Mom hadn't wanted anyone else to lose a loved one, but there'd been no other injuries. Just Perry.

Abbi's eyes burned and she swallowed hard. During the dark days after recovering from their loss, Mom had gone into tirades about a mistake the army must've made that had led to Perry's death. It had been covered up, hush-hush. Abbi had listened to several discussions about what could've happened, what might've been left unsaid. They'd even demanded answers but had been told the same story over and over again.

She picked up the corner of the curtains and let the worn, old material slide through her fingers. Cash and Dillon had come back to their own lives, like everyone else who'd served with Perry. Could she blame them? Maybe a little, but no longer. In the end, her brother was gone and never coming back.

A hot tear slid down her cheek. She hastily wiped it away as Cash said good-bye to whoever was on the phone.

He stayed in the kitchen, but a pan banged louder than normal. She didn't go in. Her eyes were probably a bit bloodshot. She had no wish to discuss what she'd been thinking about.

"Everything okay?" she called.

"For me, yeah. For my mom that just called and asked why I didn't try to talk Sissy out of joining the navy, no. And not for my dad, who asked why my mom couldn't call and tell him herself and who was the guy she moved in with."

Ugh. Why did they have to go through him for all their drama? "Sounds like a delightful conversation." Squinting, she looked for any reflection for herself in the window, but no luck. She went to the kitchen anyway, following the smell of bacon and eggs. "But Hannah called your mom at least."

"More like Mom got it out of her."

"Did you tell your dad to ask for himself who the new dude was?"

He grimaced. "No, because I don't even want to know." Her face must've registered surprise because he added, "I want her happy. I don't want specifics. Besides, it's just weird."

"I understand. But they're all adults and you don't need to be protecting them."

He shrugged noncommittally and dished up their plates.

"The sun's out and for once, the wind hasn't picked up. Want to sit on the back deck?"

She went outside with him and over breakfast she mentioned some of her ideas for paint colors and home improvements.

"Knock yourself out."

A warm glow ignited in her belly. "But was there anything you didn't like?"

He shook his head. "What do I know about any of it? You'd do better than me. And it needs it."

"You have to live in it every day, though."

They both fell silent. Her statement highlighted the unknown at the end of her vacation.

He spoke first. "What's going to happen after you go home?"

"I'll tolerate my parents' intrusion into my life until I can find my own place. Then work at the bank until I can find something that doesn't kill my soul."

She'd said it with a smile, but Cash's expression remained introspective. "And we keep seeing each other?"

"It's only an eight-hour drive." Her voice sounded empty. Only *eight* hours.

"I could go there and visit."

She nodded. "And I could come up here."

They fell quiet again.

Cash picked up his napkin and folded it. "Any chance…" He gave his head a shake.

"Any chance, what?"

He seemed at a loss for words for a minute, then met her gaze. "My roots are here. It's not fair to ask you to move, but is there a chance that someday, you'd be willing to move to Moore…to here?"

Her heart soared and she wanted to say *Yes! How's now sound?* but she couldn't bring herself to prove everyone right about how impulsive she was. Still, she couldn't keep the smile off her face. "I think there's a good chance."

Warmth infused his gaze, until it turned to smoldering heat. "The dishes can wait."

She bit her lip and stood, sliding her hand into his. Giddiness filled her from head to toe. Nothing was going to ruin this day.

CHAPTER 16

The cows were moving in one large group in the right direction. Cash finally let himself relax for a minute. He'd been doing this every year, in the spring and fall. These cows knew the drill and the promise of new food, but it didn't mean that shit couldn't happen. But. They couldn't have picked a calmer day to start moving cattle. After he'd untangled himself from Abbi's soft body, he'd called Aaron to see if he could help move one of the smaller herds and get a jump on things for the weekend.

That'd give him more time with Abbi before she went back home.

His chest tightened. He didn't like the idea of her not being around. She brought so much color to his world, not just with her mad home improvements skills. As the foundation for his family, he had little support. Lately, though, he wasn't so much foundation as the glue keeping the four of them from ripping apart and scattering to the winds.

What would family get-togethers be like? Would Mom even come back? This was her family, but only in-laws really. He was her son, but...

Cash coughed as his throat suddenly grew thick. Well, Mom wouldn't need him anymore as a go-between as she slowly cut off her soon to be ex-husband. Sissy wouldn't be coming back to Moore for years while she served in the navy.

Cash adjusted his hat as fear raced through him. Fuck, was he a twenty-nine-year-old man crying about his mommy?

Yeah, he kind of was.

But if Abbi was around, however much of their relationship Mom wanted to keep…it'd be all right.

Aaron and his gelding, Twitty—short for Conway Twitty—fell into step beside Cash. "I hear you and that girl are still seeing each other."

"Abbi, and yes. She'll have to go back home soon, but eventually, you know…"

"Nice. She seemed nice. And she can put up with you, so…" Aaron chuckled when Cash flipped him off. "Hey, if she's got any single cousins, have her bring 'em out."

Cash smiled, but his moment of relaxation was stained with sympathy. Aaron had a hard time dating and keeping a girl. His family relied on him too much, and while he was a couple of years younger than Cash, he was at the age where women ran fast when they met a guy like that. "You'll find someone, Aaron. Maybe Travis can be your wingman."

Aaron snorted and his horse nickered. "Travis is nursing his broken heart too much to think about dating."

"Good thing he didn't marry her, though." Cash winced to himself. Travis's situation wasn't much different than Cash's in that he'd found a city girl. But his ex couldn't bring herself to downgrade to the country and she'd never seemed as comfortable around their family and property. Unlike Abbi.

A clear blue sky stretched over him and his land. Things were looking up. It seemed like a fantasy to roll out of bed after a night with the sexiest girl he'd ever met, go out and do what he loved, then come home, back into her arms. But he was living the dream today.

His phone rang and he tugged it out of his pocket. Aaron trotted off with Twitty to give Cash privacy.

Cash's optimism wavered.

"Hi, Dad."

"Can you tell your mom I need to talk with her?"

Cash rolled his gaze skyward. "She's not answering?"

Dad released a gusty breath. "No. She needs to act like an adult about this. We shouldn't have to go through our lawyers for everything."

She probably worried that he'd sway her just like he had for the last thirty-plus years. "I can let her know, but I can't make promises about whether she'll talk with you."

"I appreciate it. I'm worried about her and this new man."

Cash repressed a sigh. Dad could've worried a little more before it got to this point. Cash disconnected but didn't feel like talking to Mom just yet. He texted her and pocketed his phone. His cattle and Abbi were much better subjects to dwell on.

His phone rang again.

Seriously… "Hey, Sissy."

"Oh. My. God. Mom and Dad have been on me for hours."

"What did you think they'd do with the news?"

"Let me make my own damn decisions."

Cash couldn't hold back this sigh. "Your past decision-making hasn't impressed them. They're worried. They'll get over it. Look on the bright side: when you ship out, they won't be able to get ahold of you."

"That kind of makes me feel better. Didn't you tell them that I talked to the recruiter and everything's set up, that it's my decision?"

At least ten times. "Yes, and they were upset I didn't hold your hand all the way through. Look, Sissy, the best way to show them you're serious is to do it and be the best sailor you can be. If you regret it, own it and finish your enlistment."

"Yeah, but can you tell them to quit bugging me?"

As if that would help. "Sure, but I can't make any promises." Hadn't he just said that?

"Tell them that I'm serious. I have a good feeling about the navy."

"You know, you can tell them yourself."

"I did, but they'll listen to you."

"I'll talk to them again." Lord knew, both Mom and Dad would surely call by the end of the day. He scanned the pasture. He and Aaron were nearing the corrals where Travis waited on his bay, Reba, and Abbi perched on the thick corral poles. She waved to Cash. "I gotta go, Sissy. Just don't worry about it, I'll take care of it."

For the next hour, they could call all they wanted, but Cash wasn't going to answer. He grinned at Abbi and brought Patsy Cline to a trot.

Abbi fisted her reins and glanced around. Gorgeous men surrounded her, all astride beautiful beasts.

God, could this be her life? Of course, she wasn't attracted to any of them other than Cash, who stuck close to her on Patsy Cline. The four cousins he ran the Walker Five with had arrived this morning and now surrounded the eighty cows they were driving to their winter pasture. Abbi had even gotten to meet the dark-haired cousin's fiancée. Cash had asked if Josie was going to help with the cattle drive and the exotic beauty had laughed and said there was a driveshaft calling her name. Then she'd winked at Brock and driven off in her muscle car.

And when Abbi had said she would love to drive a car like that, Cash had asked Brock. His cousin had said to stop over and Josie would take her out.

So she was helping with a real-life cattle drive, albeit a short one, and then she'd get to go drive a Mustang.

How fucking cool was that?

And these guys *lived* this life. And Cash wanted her to be a part of his life.

She couldn't fight her grin.

"Fun, isn't it?"

She glanced at Cash. Not only was he drool-worthy sitting astride his horse, but his posture was textbook. Wide shoulders, straight back, head held high. She looked at Dillon, Brock, Aaron, and Travis. All the same. Their hips rocked with their horses' movements, their heads swiveled as they checked on cattle, ball caps pulled down low, but they rode with confidence.

And she was one of them! Minus the ball cap.

"This is so fun."

Cash's easy smile warmed her from the inside out. She had been about to mount him after they ate breakfast, but Dillon had arrived, judiciously honking the horn as he'd rounded the house. Abbi had dived back into her jeans and Cash had tucked himself back into his own pants.

They were so going to pick up where they had left off once this cattle business was done.

She dutifully followed her rancher wherever he went. Soon, the herd was nestled into their winter pasture and probably just in time. Her cheeks must be pink from the brisk wind. It was fall, but this was the time of year when clouds could dump surprising amounts of snow. Not today, though.

She steered Mandrell into the barn and dismounted with the rest.

"Most of the horses winter here, too," Cash explained as he handed her a brush. "Travis keeps Reba and his siblings' horses in one of his pastures."

Brushing Mandrell, Abbi listened to the guys discuss what herd they'd move tomorrow, the weather forecast, and how they'd coordinate their weekend schedules.

"After the cattle are moved, we should have a big barbeque," Travis said. "We can do it at my place this time. Michelle was just talking about our infamous grills."

Cash stopped brushing and rested his forearms on Patsy Cline's back. "You two back together?"

Abbi thought she was done brushing, but feeling a slight increase in tension, she kept up her long strokes and Mandrell didn't complain.

Travis rose to his full height, which was just as tall as Cash. "Yeah, and I don't need to hear it."

"Hear what?"

All the guys stopped to watch the interaction while Travis elaborated. "How you think I can do better than Michelle."

"I never said that. And it's not about Michelle, it's about you two breaking up and getting back together again —again."

Abbi stroked Mandrell as quietly as she could. Would the guys start pointing at her and asking what Cash was doing with her?

"Whatever," Travis grumbled. "I'm not asking permission to date my fiancée."

Cash made a disgusted sound only she heard.

Aaron spoke up. "Why do we have to wait until we're

done moving cattle? Let's go out tonight. Barley 'n' Hops has live music tonight."

"I'd love to take Elle out dancing," Dillon spoke quickly, like he was glad to move on from the Michelle subject.

Abbi glanced around at all the men. Belonging to this family would be like gaining four other brothers. And a sister. Not to mention the other cousins Abbi hadn't met yet.

"I could ask Josie," Brock said.

Cash looked at her with a question in his eyes and she grinned.

"Sounds fun."

Abbi laughed as Cash spun her around the dance floor. The man was as good on his feet as he was in bed. She didn't miss the envious, sometimes seething looks she got from women. Cash hadn't let go of her all night.

Loud country music kicked a steady beat through the bar. Men and women Abbi's age and older crowded the tables and dance floor. The place was just what Abbi would expect in a small town: wood beams, booths, and tables lining the dance area, and a polished hardwood floor. It was homey, but fancy enough to make going out a treat.

"Are you thirsty, honey?" He had to yell in her ear as close as they were to the band.

She nodded, and he led her back to the table their group sat at when they weren't out dancing. Abbi chose a seat and spotted Dillon and his beautiful girlfriend two-stepping to the current song. Josie looked like she struggled at dancing as much as Abbi had, but like Cash, Brock was a pro at gliding with her across the floor. Travis and Michelle seemed like they were in perfect sync, and Aaron had found a few single ladies—for dance partners at least.

She let her gaze wander to the bar to pick out Cash. With his height and broad shoulders, it wasn't hard. Neither was seeing the lady next to him, pressing against his side. She was cute and dressed to kill. Her flirty mannerisms were all for Cash. Abbi watched, more amused than irritated.

The woman murmured to him and he shook his head. The bartender slid a pitcher toward him and he smoothly snatched it up, gave the woman a nod of polite dismissal, and swaggered back to Abbi.

Abbi's grin grew as he slid into the seat next to her. "Am I going to have to come with and protect you next time?"

"Yes, please. I said no three times." He smirked with a hint of apology. "She's not used to that, from me or anyone else."

"She'll get over it. Aaron's the only one of you guys free."

"Don't mention that around him." Cash poured their beer. "He's got a thing about not dating anyone the rest of us…you know."

"Does that leave him anyone under the age of sixty?"

Cash hesitated, then chuckled. "We weren't that bad."

"You weren't?" She moved like she was going to stand. "Let me go ask that girl who was hitting on you."

"You could." He grabbed her and dragged her onto his lap. "Or you could sit here and talk about the next thing that comes up." He nuzzled her neck.

"Oh my god, I haven't heard that line for years."

His gentle laugh sent shivers up and down her spine. "I know a place where we could…talk."

She met his hot gaze. "I'd like to talk."

They were in his vehicle within minutes and cruising through town.

Abbi had a hard time fighting her grin. When had she looked forward to having sex before? Not just *ooh, I'm getting some* but *yes! I'm getting some!* It seemed to be more every time she was with Cash. "Do I get to see a part of Moore I haven't yet?"

"Uh…I was going to take you to the lake we went fishing at, but I can find another spot."

"No, the lake is good. We can do another spot another time."

He shot her a sidelong glance. "Yes, ma'am."

She gazed out her window as they bumped along the small gravel road. The only light came from the pickup's headlights and the occasional yard light visible through the trees.

"It's so dark out here. I've never seen this many stars."

"It's why I wanted to take you to the lake. The road out there is decent and there's little light pollution. I used to go there when I was a teen and Mom and Dad were fighting. I'd throw a blanket in the bed of the pickup and stretch out to think."

Her heart went out to the young Cash who'd felt responsible for his parents' problems. "You don't have to be alone to deal with it anymore."

He gave her a warm look. "I appreciate it, but you don't need to deal with my family drama."

"I mean it, Cash. I don't want to be coddled—I want us to be partners. You don't need to protect me from anything. I can handle it." She'd never again be part of a relationship where her man made decisions for her own good.

He patted her knee and ran his hand up her thigh. "I'll always protect you."

His words seemed to echo with a deeper meaning, but she shook her head. "No. We're in this together. Don't baby me."

His expression became serious. "I won't."

"Promise?" She'd make him pinky swear if she had to.

"Of course." His charming smile should've eased her sudden anxiety about jumping in with another boyfriend who didn't think of her as an equal. But she'd seen that smile before.

Why wouldn't he be one hundred percent genuine? No, she wasn't going to second-guess his word. He'd been nothing but real with her and tonight was about enjoying them and their new standing as a solid couple.

CHAPTER 17

*H*is house came into view. The yard light cast a soft glow over all the buildings on his property. Cash had taken her to the lake, but with the cool temps, they'd had to scurry back into the cab of his truck. Quick sex in the backseat of his truck had only been an appetizer.

He'd gone out dancing with her and now he got to take her home. A guy could get used to this.

No, he'd never get used to it. Not when it was what he'd wanted for so long but had told himself he wasn't good enough to have. He'd been the plus-one several times as his cousins had dated. Then witnessed Dillon find true love. And Brock—the least likely of them to find a woman who understood him—as he fell hard for Josie. Each time, it'd bothered Cash more and more that he wasn't allowed to have that.

But he was. And she was next to him. She wanted him to be honest with her. And he would, but not about her brother. It'd devastate her; she'd blame herself for ever making her brother worry.

He shot her a grin full of promise as he turned into his drive.

She smiled back and when her gaze angled away, she frowned. "What the hell?"

He looked in the same direction and an ominous cloud floated over the whole night. A dark sedan sat in front of his garage, parked next to Abbi's car.

"Is that Ellis's car?"

She nodded, but she was squinting to look inside the vehicle. All at once, three doors opened.

He recognized Ellis as he stepped out of the car, but there was another man and a woman with him.

"Who are they?" he asked.

"My parents."

Ice washed through his veins. The air around them grew heavy. Abbi must be thinking the same thing he was. This couldn't be good.

"Haven't you talked to them since you told your ex off?"

She shook her head, her gaze stuck on the people congregated behind the car, waiting for Cash to park. "I thought he'd go home, and I just didn't want to deal with them. I texted them and said I was staying in Moore until the end of the week and then I'd love their help moving my stuff."

Since Ellis the Ex was in Cash's normal parking spot, he swung around in front of his separate garage.

Abbi gave him one final look, as if she was siphoning strength from him to face her family.

As soon as she got out, her mom's voice carried across the yard. "Abigail, thank god!"

Cash's boots hit the ground in time to see Abbi's mom scurry across the gravel, her arms out to hug her daughter.

Abbi let her mom soothe herself for a moment. "What are you guys doing here?"

Abbi's dad strode to his ladies, his suspicious glare landing on Cash. Cash looked at Ellis. The man's grim stare was stuck on Abbi, like if he didn't look at Cash, Cash didn't exist.

"When Ellis called and told us you broke up with him because of..." Mrs. Daniels peered at Cash.

He stopped by his tailgate and waited, letting Abbi take the reins in this situation.

"Mom, Dad, this is Cash Walker. Perry called him Reno."

Mr. Daniels's jaw clenched and he assessed Abbi's ruffled hair and rumpled appearance. Cash's own shirt was untucked and his coat was in the cab. They didn't look like a couple who'd been out dancing. They looked like they'd been doing what they'd just done.

"Nice to meet you." Cash put out his hand. Mr. Daniels glowered at it, but eventually grasped it in a firm handshake. Mr. Daniels was an older, more mature version of Perry Daniels. Cash could hardly look at him without being assaulted by memories of joking with Daniels—or of finding him staring at his weapon while deep in thought, huge lines of sadness etched into his face.

He tried to look up again, but seeing Mrs. Daniels sent a wave of grief over him. These people had lost a son, and no matter how much Cash told himself he wasn't responsible, he'd always feel like a failure for not having prevented Daniels's decision. What had Abbi said? Her parents had been hurt and disappointed that none of Daniels's squad had come to visit after they'd gotten home.

Cash had known why he hadn't made the trip, but now he *knew*. He hadn't felt worthy enough to face them. Their fear and grief over Abbi's actions likely couldn't compare to what their son's death had done to them. He wouldn't have been able to stammer out an apology and lurch away. And how would that have sat with them?

"What's going on here?" Mr. Daniels asked gruffly.

The man must've taken Cash's avoidance as guilt that he

had ill intentions toward Abbi.

Abbi broke away from her mom and crossed to Cash's side. He hooked an arm around her and forced himself to face Daniels's parents—Abbi's parents.

"I met Cash and we've formed a relationship. I don't know what Ellis told you, *how* he told you, but there's nothing nefarious. Being with Cash helped me see how miserable I was at home."

Mr. Daniels scowled. "You ended a four-year relationship and started another one within a week?"

"Abigail," Mrs. Daniels breathed, "what were you think-ing? Do you know how worried we've been?"

Remorse touched Abbi's eyes. "I kept telling you I was fine. I really am."

"Why would you—" Abbi's mom drew herself up. "I think we should talk in private."

Abbi shook her head and pressed close to Cash. "We will all discuss this together, not that I need to justify anything I've done. I'm an adult."

Her dad's forehead creased in concern. "Fine. Then why would you leave a man who treats you like a queen, provides for you, and came running after you for a coward who can't face his friends' parents?"

Cash recoiled. Whoa. Direct attack. But no anger flurried within him. Daniels's parents were right to think he was a coward.

"Dad!"

"No, it's all right." Cash rubbed her shoulder.

Abbi's mom went to stand by her husband, her expression strained. "Ellis told us he asked around town about Cash."

Cash wanted to groan. With his own history fueled by his dad's actions, he could imagine what had been said about him.

"And what, Mom? You're going to believe Ellis and a

bunch of strangers over what I say?"

"You haven't made the best decisions in the past," her mom said.

"He has quite a reputation." Mr. Daniels's hard stare burned into Cash. "He's not someone I want my daughter with."

Cash chewed on his cheek. He couldn't exactly argue with the man. He'd worked hard to dissuade anyone from thinking he was boyfriend material. Abbi squeezed his side in reassurance.

"He's a hard-working man," Abbi defended. "He works from sunup to sundown." She shot Ellis a hard look as if to stress that Cash worked longer hours than him. "Hard, honest work. I'm sure there's plenty of places in Moore I could find a job."

Her mom's eyes bugged out. "You're moving here?"

"Eventually."

Ellis drifted toward them, hesitancy in his step. "I accept that you and I are done, Abigail. But it doesn't mean I don't care about you. Before you give up your entire life, think about what kind of living he makes from ranching, how unreliable it can be."

He had a feeling about where Ellis was going with this. "My cousins and I run a successful farming and ranching operation, which I'm sure you discovered when you asked around town."

"And when grain prices fall?" Ellis countered. "Or cattle prices? What if a hail storm wipes out your crops? Do you have any education to fall back on, or will the whole operation crash?"

Abbi stiffened next to him and it was his turn to give her a reassuring squeeze.

"Do I have a college degree? That's what you're asking, right? No. I don't." He directed his next words to the worried mom and dad hovering in his yard. "Rest assured, this business is one of the longest running in the county. I'm a fifth-generation farmer and rancher, and this place has weathered many storms, both climate related and financial."

"Doesn't mean you're the man for my daughter," her dad said calmly. "Abigail, why would you want to be one of many?"

Cash sucked in a breath. It was hard not to get pissed, but more at himself because what the man said about his past was true. A previous lack of commitment didn't make him a bad guy. He hadn't lied to the women he'd been with, or made false promises.

"Cash's past is none of my business, and what goes on between us is none of your business—" she stabbed a finger at them, then pointed at Ellis, "—and none of yours."

Her mom spoke and her voice was low, serious. "Perry told me plenty about Reno—Cash—whatever the hell you call yourself. Despite the stories, like my daughter, my son seemed to treasure your friendship. Yet you let him down. You let us down. You let him get killed, and you let the army lie to us and blame my son—" her voice cracked, "—who's no longer here to defend himself. I won't tolerate my daughter associating with a man like you."

Cash worked to steady his breathing. Fucking Daniels wasn't here to defend himself and his parents blamed Cash for the man taking his own life. Actions that would lead to Cash losing the love of his life. Or worse, having her lose her parents because he didn't tell them what had really happened.

Abbi would walk. He could feel her resolve in the hard lines of her body. She was prepared to leave everything in Green Bay and set up life with him. She'd lost her brother. They'd lost a son. Cash couldn't be responsible for them losing a daughter, too.

"The army didn't lie."

Abbi nodded next to him, and his heart cracked. Would she hate him when this was over?

Her mom cut a hand through the air. "No. I know they did. Why was my son taken and no one else was even injured?"

There were injuries, but nothing severe, and definitely not a loss of life. "Because he disobeyed orders to fall back. Dil—my cousin relayed the order and we were working our way back out when I noticed Daniels wasn't with me."

Mrs. Daniels shook her head. "You're lying. Protecting yourself. I knew you were hiding something. Perry wouldn't have put himself in danger like that."

"Mom, you don't even know what you're talking about. It was an accident."

Mrs. Daniels charged him. "No! My son was killed because you made a mistake. You left him behind."

"He was depressed." The rest of Cash's breath froze in his lungs. He'd said it. He'd only confessed it once, to Dillon several months ago, but now he was telling the people he'd sworn never to tell.

Mrs. Daniels gasped and drew up short. Abbi disengaged herself from his hold and peered up at him.

Cash shoved a hand through his hair. All those shitty nights of sleep and it hadn't been the actual experience plaguing him, but the helpless feeling that had preceded it. He'd turned around and Daniels's vest and Kevlar helmet had disappeared around a corner, into a room they'd just reported an IED in.

He sucked in a shallow breath and let it spill. "Daniels had been mentioning things here and there, like how he felt powerless to help you guys out and even if he got out of the army, he'd be no use. He just wanted to—" Cash shrugged weakly, "—help. He wanted to mean something and he'd been getting reckless, but I never thought— God, I'm so sorry, I would've dragged him out if I'd known he was going to go back in and kill…"

Cash couldn't bring himself to say it. And he had a hard time not hating Daniels right now for putting him in this position.

Abbi's face went ashen. "Perry killed himself."

Cash ducked his head and it was all he could do to hold her gaze. "Yes. I didn't say anything at the time because I was afraid of being wrong. I was afraid of being right. I was afraid of how much worse your family would take it if you knew it was intentional."

No one moved except Ellis, who walked up behind Abbi's parents and laid a hand on each of them.

"The money that paid off my school," Abbi said woodenly. A strangled cry wrenched from her and tears welled in her eyes. "He thought his death would be better for me?"

She sobbed, seemed to try to hold it in, but another followed. Her mother silently wept behind her and her dad's gaze was planted on the ground.

"He was depressed. It wasn't your fault."

"My son suffered from depression and no one helped him." Mr. Daniels's stricken tone cut Cash in two.

"We didn't know. It wasn't until afterward that I put it all together."

Abbi's dad speared him with a hard glare. "Because you were too busy having a good time."

Cash bit down on his tongue. There was no hooking up or partying in Iraq. It was the most responsible he'd been in his life. But nothing he said would make any of them feel better.

"Why didn't you tell me?" Abbi's ragged whisper barely cut through her tears.

"I wanted to protect you from it."

She snarled. "You promised you wouldn't do that!"

"Not about this, Abbi. I couldn't let you blame yourself for this."

She shoved her hair back and rolled her eyes skyward. "It wasn't your decision to make. I came here to find out what happened to Perry. You knew that and you still didn't tell me."

No, he hadn't. And if he had to do it over again, he wouldn't have told any of them. The pain rolling off them was too much. He should've found another way to help Abbi's relationship with her parents.

"You *promised*." Her eyes glistened.

"I couldn't do that to you."

She spun on her heel and stormed to the house. "I'm getting my things."

What? "Wait."

She kept walking.

"Abbi!"

He trotted after her, past her dad and her mom crying on his shoulder, past Ellis. He looked as haggard as the rest of them. Couldn't he at least look smug, give Cash a reason to hate him?

Cash barged into the house after his girlfriend.

"No." Abbi didn't even look over her shoulder as she charged into his bedroom and started throwing her things into her bag. "I'm not your mom and dad. I'm not Hannah. I'm not going to be babied like all the others in your life."

"This is different. Your brother's problems were way more serious than any of my family drama."

She slammed the top closed. "Exactly. The most important thing you should've shared with me, and you kept it secret. You didn't think I could handle it. I refuse to be treated like the rest of your family, and I refuse to be treated like I have been by everyone else in my life."

"I knew you'd blame yourself for what your brother did. I couldn't have you do that."

"You're not listening!" she yelled. "That's not your choice. Of course I blame myself. But now I have the truth and I can work on healing." She waved her hand between them. "But this is broken."

"What are you saying?"

"I'm saying that I'm going home." She hauled her bag up and grabbed her tote and pushed past him out the door.

Outside, her dad waited by the trunk and her mom was already in Ellis's car with Ellis at the wheel.

Cash followed her all the way to the back of the car. "You're leaving, just like that? Can't we talk about this?"

She dropped her luggage and whirled on him. "I gave you plenty of chances to talk. Plenty. I *begged*. And yet you lied."

Her dad loaded the bags and went around to open the back door for her.

"I'm sorry. I really am. I didn't realize how—"

"No, you didn't, and I think that's worse. I confided in you, and you ignored how important it was to me." She closed the distance to the open door and turned to face him. He stood back, his feet anchored to the driveway. "I really fell for you. But I can't do this if I'm going to just be another person in your life to coddle."

She handed her car keys to her dad. "I'll ride with Mom."

She slid into the backseat with her mother; her dad shut the door. With one last hard look at Cash, he marched to Abbi's car and got in.

Ellis backed around and drove off. Abbi was collapsed on her mom's shoulder and they clung to each other. Cash watched them until they disappeared into the night with Abbi's car trailing behind.

She'd left him. He wanted to call his mom and tell her she'd been right all along. He was no good for anyone.

ash swayed with Patsy Cline's steps. The bitter wind bit his face as he scowled at the line of cattle in front of him. He ducked his head down into the collar of his jacket. Snow was in the forecast for the week and since it was early November, the amounts could vary from a dusting to a full-fledged blizzard despite what the weather reported.

Another horse drew up next to him. Dillon on LeDoux. The two horses nickered at each other.

"I thought you'd look happier. This is the last herd we have to bring in." Dillon had been a little smarter and wore a stocking hat and heavier gloves than the worn work gloves Cash wore.

"It'll be nice to get out of the wind." The tip of his nose had lost feeling an hour ago and his fingers hurt from being cold. Kind of how Cash had felt the last two weeks.

"Haven't heard from her yet?"

Cash ground his teeth, couldn't bring himself to shake his head. "She's a champion at not answering her phone."

"She's grieving. Give her time."

"She said she was done with me." Some nights, he was tempted to jump in his truck and cruise to Green Bay. But chasing after her hadn't worked for her ex.

"She probably thought she was, too. But finding out Perry killed himself is a whole new heartache to process." Dillon dipped his gaze to LeDoux's head. "I should've gone there and talked to his parents."

"You didn't know what he'd done." If Dillon had, his drinking after he'd gotten home might've been worse.

"No, but I could've talked to them. At least eased their minds that they weren't getting told fabricated stories."

"If you want to go the shoulda route, then I should've recognized Perry was suicidal. I was closer to him than the rest of the guys."

"Would you really have known?" When Cash didn't say anything, Dillon continued. "We didn't know, Cash. And we can't go back and make ourselves know."

"Did I do the wrong thing by not telling her?" Because it sure didn't feel like it. Cash had absorbed all the grief that had spilled off her parents that night. He could've prevented that. He could've still had Abbi with him. "Was I selfish, telling them? I thought Abbi was going to quit talking to her family over how they were talking to me."

"I can't really say what's right or wrong, but I talked to Elle." Dillon spoke cautiously as if he was afraid how Cash would react.

Cash didn't care. If Dillon needed to talk to someone, a mental health professional for a girlfriend couldn't hurt. "What'd she say?"

Dillon sighed. "The whole situation was bad, there's no way around it. She never really came out and said either way —counselors are kinda like that. But she felt that the Daniels knowing the truth would help them heal and move on. Same with Abbi. They weren't making progress before; maybe now they can. But what's between you and Abbi has nothing to do with her brother."

He was afraid of that. Just like he was afraid there was nothing between him and Abbi anymore.

Abbi stood in her empty efficiency apartment. It smelled like stale smoke and citrus cleaner. The linoleum she stood on was yellowed with age and the matted carpet to her left would be better off if it was rolled up and used to build a bonfire.

Cash and his cousins had talked about building a bonfire after they finished moving cattle. Had they?

None of her business.

She released a slow breath and thought of the boxes in her parents' garage she had to load up and haul here. Ugh. Would her belongings pick up the scent of this place?

Home.

She wanted to run. But this dingy, old, rundown apartment signified her future.

She jumped at a tap on the door.

"Sorry to startle you, kiddo." Dad came in. Was she going to get a lecture about how she'd kept it unlocked?

To be fair, they hadn't lectured her much in the last month and a half. They hadn't done much other than mourn Perry all over again.

More guilt piled on. Not just for her brother. She missed Cash terribly, and in the six weeks since she'd walked out on him, the feeling hadn't abated.

He'd tried calling, but not since the early days after she'd holed up in her parents' house and left only to do a zombie act through work.

Had she done the right thing?

Yes.

No.

Maybe.

She'd been about to relent and call Cash when Mom had started in about Ellis. Nope. None of that again. Abbi had zoomed straight for the classifieds and found this swanky joint. The previous renter had had to serve time and couldn't make payments. The owner had trashed his stuff and opened it back up to rent. She'd gotten a deal on the deposit.

Dad set the box on the counter. Her favorite dishware. They had fishes on them.

They looked kinda like the trout she'd caught with Cash.

Argh. She had to quit doing that!

"You didn't have to bring my stuff, Dad."

"I know you said you could do it all yourself, but it doesn't mean you have to." Dad paused to shrug out of his winter coat. "But you can help haul them up those stairs and I won't complain." He looked around the place and grimaced.

Yeah, it was that bad. The state of her living conditions meant she couldn't leave her job. Responsible Abbi was in full force. Working at a job that killed her creative soul but paid for a smelly roof over her head was her life.

"You didn't have to move out."

"I did. You two wouldn't treat me like an adult if I stayed."

"Abbi—"

"Dad."

He fell quiet.

"I'll go grab a load." She spun toward the door.

"You've changed."

She stopped and nodded. "You and Mom always said I had to grow up."

"We worried about you. You're a free spirit. Were a free

spirit. I thought Perry's death just affected you so much that you lost your energy, but that's not what happened, was it?"

"No, that's exactly what happened. How could I keep making you two lose sleep when you've suffered enough?"

A sad smile crossed his face. "I'm not going to lie, I'd rather have an unhappy daughter than have to bury you." Her heart twisted as she recalled her mother breaking down over Perry's casket. "But it'd be my greatest wish if you could be both alive and happy."

She'd been so terribly happy with Cash, until he'd betrayed her trust—her one wish in a relationship. The anger fueling her righteousness was harder and harder to muster. Had it been the shock of the truth of Perry's death that had caused her to feel so betrayed?

Did it matter anymore? Six weeks was a long time to move on. She hadn't, but he might've, or even slipped back into his old ways.

A chasm's worth of sadness opened up. She'd lost him. She'd told him they were done and yet he'd tried—until he hadn't.

Hot tears spilled down her cheeks, and she rushed out the door. Cold Wisconsin air hit her face. She sniffled and wiped the tears away. Digging around in the trunk of Dad's car, she picked a box to haul. When she straightened and turned, she jumped. He was right behind her.

Great. He'd heard her crying.

She dropped her gaze and rushed past him. She thought he might stop her, but instead he selected another box from her pitiful pile of belongings.

They trudged up the stairs and went out for another load. Dad didn't make small talk as they finished unloading his car.

"It's just your closet and what's in the dressers that need to be hauled over." He gave her a pointed look. "Take the dressers. They're yours if you want them."

Her first instinct was to say no, but she should swallow her pride if it meant not living out of laundry baskets. "Thanks."

He rubbed the back of his neck and her heart sank. It was his "I don't want to talk about this but as your dad, I should" move.

"You've been crying a lot lately. Is it about Ellis or Perry?"

The easy answer would be to say yes. He would understand and drop the subject. But part of being treated as an adult was to be true to herself.

"No." Didn't mean she had to spill every humiliating detail.

"That friend of Perry's, Reno?"

That name *so* did not fit him. "Cash, yes. I miss him. But it's over."

His mouth formed a hard line of disapproval. "I was surprised, as close as you claimed to be when we were out there…well, he didn't come running after you."

"He called. A lot."

His brows lifted. "Really? But he didn't come down."

"I never answered. I was so furious, but…"

"But you're not now."

She shook her head, tears threatening to well. "It's been over a month since he last tried. It's over."

"You two didn't know each other long." He said it like that explained it all, as if what she felt had just been a fluke.

"No, we didn't." She turned back to unload her meager stash of books.

"But he made you happy?"

"Yes, because he made me feel like myself."

"Is he really a good guy?"

She whirled around. "It doesn't matter. It's over. And like you and Mom—" and freaking Ellis, "—pointed out, we didn't know each other long." But while she had known him, he'd been the biggest, most genuine gentleman she'd ever met.

Dad didn't reply, but he helped her with the rest of her boxes.

He threw her a concerned look before he left. She forced herself to smile and wave, then sighed when the door shut and went back to sort her items.

She found the sketch pad she'd used to draw Alfalfa. Opening it was a bad idea, but she did it anyway. Scribbled over the page were the fine lines that outlined the cat and the harsher lines of the porch slats. She turned the page and her hand dropped away. Cash's stick-figure drawing of the cat made her giggle. She choked back a sob.

Questions flooded her. The same ones she'd been asking herself for six weeks. Had she done the right thing? Would things with him have worked out? Or would he have eventually started picking and choosing what he shared with her.

She folded herself onto the floor, her legs crossed, the sketch pad on her lap. How long she stared at the drawing, she didn't know, but finally she rummaged around her items until she found a pencil. She turned the page and began a new sketch, letting the pencil flow, not consciously controlling what she drew.

Not surprisingly, the outline of a man's face formed. She spent the most time on the eyes, perfecting the intensity with a touch of his ever-constant good humor.

When she was done, a decent rendition of Cash stared back at her. Even as an amateur, she'd been able to capture his personality, the classic handsomeness of his features.

No, they hadn't known each other for long, but it sure seemed like she'd known him better than she'd known anyone in her life.

With a disgusted snarl, she popped up and tossed the pad

and pencil in a bottom drawer in her kitchen and kicked it shut.

CHAPTER 19

Cash was man enough to admit he was hiding in the kitchen. They'd gathered for Christmas at Dillon's house and the rest of his family was oohing and aahing over Elle's shiny new engagement ring.

He was ecstatic for his cousin, and he loved Elle like a sister, but the sappy, happy mess made him want to vomit. He couldn't even nurse a beer because Dillon's house was dry. Their relatives never brought wine or alcoholic beverages to his cousin's place no matter how many times he assured him it'd be all right.

He searched for something to do, but food lined the counters and flatware was laid out. Everything was ready for them to eat, after everyone got over the love-fest. Could he eat and rush home, where he could watch football without fielding any questions? Every time one of his cousins broached the topic of Abbi, or worse, how he should move on, Cash cut them off. He couldn't even sneak away on Patsy Cline and just ride horse all day because there was two feet of snow on the ground.

The only time he allowed himself to think about Abbi was

when he left his phone in a drawer when he went to work for the day. She'd been good at ignoring calls, and he'd taken notes. His sister was shipping out for navy boot camp soon and his parents were constantly bitching to him—about her, about each other, about the divorce.

Who knew as an adult he'd have to referee who spent Christmas where?

Hannah's squeal of delight reached him. The sound trampled his last nerve. Sure, she could enjoy herself because she didn't have to deal with the fallout of what she did.

He couldn't take it. He slipped through the door to the garage, stomped into his boots, and marched out into the snow. He hopped into his truck. As soon as his engine fired, everyone would know he'd left.

Merry fucking Christmas. He drove across the gravel road to his driveway and scowled at Mom's car in the drive.

She'd done what she'd promised. *I'm spending Christmas with my children.* Dad had stayed last night and planned to leave town as soon as the shindig at Dillon's was done. Or hell, stay in town with an old flame of his.

Mom must've timed her arrival so they'd all be away. Less confrontation that way.

He parked and went to the door. He stomped the snow off his boots and went inside.

Mom came out of the guest room. "What are you doing home so early?"

Ah, shit. He wasn't prepared with an answer. "I just didn't want to be there."

Concern crossed her face. "Why?"

"Just…didn't." He tried to head for the kitchen, but she blocked him.

"I think we need to talk."

He exhaled and gave her a *not now* look.

"Please." She gestured to the couch. "Sit down, Cash."

Like he was still a little boy, he trudged to sit. Mom settled into the recliner next to him.

"What really happened with Abbi?"

"I told you. I ruined it."

Her lips flattened. "Why do you think you ruined it?"

He lifted a shoulder. "Because I'm not meant for a relationship."

"Why would you think that?"

"Isn't it what you've been telling me my whole life?" More bitterness than he intended seeped out. "'Don't be like your dad. Don't get into a relationship if you're just going to hurt her.'"

She blinked, her mouth hanging open. "I was trying to teach you how to be a good man in a relationship, not that you'd be awful at them."

His gaze dropped to the floor. "Do you have any idea how what you said affected me?"

She sat forward. "Of course not! Cash, how could you think...?"

"Because of Holly. And Dad."

She was quiet for a moment. "And you felt like I resented you and made you pay, in a way, for how your father hurt me."

Cash nodded. He shouldn't have said anything. Who knows how he'd unsettled Dillon's gathering, and now he'd ruined the one at his own house.

Her sniffle jerked his head up. "Oh god, Cash. You're one of the best human beings I know. I'm proud to be your mom." Tears poured down her cheeks. She searched around for a tissue.

He scrambled up to find one for her. He wanted to believe her, but making his own mother cry on Christmas kinda negated her claim.

As he was coming back, the front door burst open.

"Cash! Where the hell are y—" Dad stopped when his gaze hit Cash. Sissy was right behind him, frowning at their sobbing mother. "Patty, what's wrong?"

Cash handed Mom the tissue and sat back down. This was going to be fun.

She blew her nose. "Nothing. Everything. I just realized I was a horrible mom." Her shoulders quaked as sobs overtook her.

"What'd you do, Cash?" Dad marched in, then stopped. He stepped forward like he wanted to comfort his soon-to-be ex-wife, but ultimately hung back.

"What'd you say, Cash?" Sissy shot him a glare and squatted by their mom. "Mom, it's okay. You're a great mom."

He might be to blame, but they'd jumped on him almost immediately. "Easy for you to say, Sissy." Cash jumped up again and stormed to the window. "Of course life was smooth for you. I was the mediator between your bullshit and Mom and Dad."

"Ca—"

He cut her off with a wave of his hand. "And I'm still doing it. You're old enough to drink. Old enough to join the military. Yet you're constantly asking me to talk to Mom and Dad for you. And you two." He shoved a hand through his hair. "I'm so sorry, Mom. You weren't a shitty mom. But I'm the kid in the relationship. You and Dad need to deal with your own issues. I can't do it anymore. Yeah, thirty might be on the horizon, but I want to think everything is hunky-dory between you two."

Mom lifted her head to stare at him with red, puffy eyes. Dad planted his hands on his hips and remained silent. Sissy gaped at him.

"And what went wrong with Abbi? She was pissed and felt betrayed when I treated her the same way I treat you all. I protected her because I thought she couldn't handle it." He spun back to the window. "And it wasn't something insignificant. I was the only one who knew her brother purposely stepped on an IED so she'd get his life insurance money. Was I wrong to keep that information from her?"

How'd he gone from bitching them out to asking for their opinion? But he had to know. Had he been wrong?

"Was I?" He sounded pathetic to his own ears. But that question robbed him of sleep, stole his peace. He'd only wanted to do right by Abbi.

"Oh…Cash…" Mom blew her nose. Sissy hit the floor, sitting cross-legged to watch him with wide eyes.

"You know that for sure. About her brother?" Dad asked.

"As sure as I can be without bringing him back from the dead to ask." He massaged a temple. "She was so upset…so hurt."

Dad shuffled across the floor to take a seat. "You kept it secret all this time? How'd she find out?"

Cash scowled. He spilled the story. How they'd met. Her ex. Why he'd never gotten serious with a girl. Abbi's parents and their accusations. When he was done, his shoulders hung and he felt like twenty years had been piled on him.

He shouldn't burden them with this, but he couldn't do it by himself anymore.

Mom spoke first. "I have to agree with Dillon. That's something only Abbi could decide, and like you found out, she wanted to know. Rather, it wasn't so much that she wanted to know, it was that she felt it was *important* to know. Does that make sense?"

He'd managed her just like his family. Even worse, he'd failed to treat her like the capable adult she was, instead joining the ranks of Ellis and everyone else who thought they knew what was best for her.

After years of being smothered by her family and her

boyfriend, Abbi had been fed up with others determining what she was fit to handle. She'd trusted him not to do that.

He let his head hang. So now he understood. And he'd still made his mom cry on Christmas.

"Just like you should've told us to handle our own problems." Mom sucked in a deep breath. "You're easy to talk to. I treasure your support, but I can see now how..." She teared up again.

"Aw, Mom. I'm sorry. I didn't mean—"

She shook her head, her brown hair flying. "No. You're right." She lifted her gaze to Dad's. "You and I need to keep this between us."

"I still want to know what's going on," Sissy piped up. "You guys have to include me, no matter how far away I am."

"We'll keep you updated." Dad's expression was troubled. But then he'd just been told his actions had fucked up not only his marriage but his son's outlook on relationships. "Cash is right. This mess is between your mom and I. I... I know what I was like and why we're getting divorced. I'll..." He looked at each one of them. "Let's just have a nice meal with all of us." He stopped on his wife. "Patty, can you tolerate me hanging around for a little while?"

Her features were carefully void of emotion. "I think it's important that we learn to enjoy family functions together. Not just for the kids, but for our own well-being. I don't want either of us to miss out."

"Me, either." Dad cleared his throat, like he might be tearing up, too. The divorce was tearing at all of them. "Cash, think we can find something to grill?"

His family had hit a huge milestone. They'd communicated honestly together for the first time since...ever. Could this be a turning point for them? Were they on their way to a new normal that was healthier than their old ways?

The first person he wanted to tell about his family's

progress was out of his reach. But if it weren't for her, this would've never happened. At least he had that.

Yeah.

That didn't make him feel better.

Dishes were piled on the table. Only a few slices of roast beef remained. Cash's family had decimated the vegetables he had left in the fridge. This was the lowest-key Christmas on record. When his family celebrated, they included everyone. And Cash missed his extended family and hanging out with his cousins, especially the ones he didn't get to see often. But he wouldn't trade this experience for anything.

There was still a heavy dose of awkwardness between Mom and Dad, but that'd decrease in time. Mom mentioned going to a divorce support group, and while the divorce was hitting Dad hard, at least he seemed to be owning his role and accepting that his life had changed.

They didn't talk about Mom's newest...boyfriend? Man-friend? Lover? Cash wanted to shudder. But they didn't talk about Dad's conquests, either. Cash, and probably Sissy, was just fine with that arrangement. If either parent's special friend turned into a significant other, then he'd want details. Until then, ignorance was bliss.

Sissy talked excitedly about the information the recruiter had given her, and Cash was content to listen. Residual sadness lingered, but he supposed he had to get used to missing Abbi.

On the flip side, his house was cleaner than it'd ever been. Since he didn't go out as much, just to bullshit with the boys, he'd had some extra nights free. He'd even finished painting all the bedrooms and had a list compiled for the lumberyard and hardware store.

A knock on the door cut off all conversation.

His parents were used to not living here anymore and Cash was the only one that rose.

He opened the front door to Dillon, Brock, Aaron, and Travis.

Oh. Yeah. He'd just walked out on Christmas dinner. Hadn't even congratulated his best friend on his engagement.

"Sorry, guys, I—"

"Back up, we're coming in," Dillon said as he stepped forward.

Okay. Cash internally prepped for confrontation number two. He moved out of the way as his cousins filed in. His parents and Sissy stood at the entrance into the living room but hung back as if they sensed the other guys' intent.

"Look, Dillon, I'm sorry I left. Congratulations, man. I'm happy for you." The sincerity was easier for Cash to get out than when he'd tried earlier. Abbi had ripped a gaping hole in his heart, but Dillon's future was important to him.

"Thanks, but we're here about you." Dillon crossed his arms. He and the others stood on the welcome mat, boots dripping melted snow into the fabric. None of them had worn coats. Cash glanced outside. Aaron's black and gray pickup was parked in the driveway.

"What about me?" They hadn't asked Sissy or his parents for privacy. Whatever it was, everyone was going to hear.

Aaron crossed his arms over his chest. "You're not much better than a ghost. We have to figure out how to get Abbi back."

So…that's why they were here. A quick little trip to rally his morale and win the love of his life back.

"Sorry, guys. I tried. She wouldn't speak to me."

Brock spoke. "But she never said she wouldn't take you back, right?"

Cash narrowed his eyes at him and shook his head.

Travis scratched his jaw. "That's the loophole. And here we thought we were going to start at ground zero."

"What the fuck are you talking about?"

Dillon answered. "When you left, we had a little brainstorming session. It's been almost two months and you haven't rebounded, you haven't moved on. Hell, I can't even say whether you're in stasis or not. You're like a ranching zombie."

Aaron's head bobbed. "You're sad, dude."

Hope rustled in his chest, but he brushed it aside. He'd called. He'd texted. Abbi hadn't answered.

Cash pinched the bridge of his nose. Getting Abbi to listen to him was only the first hurdle. Expecting her to take another chance on him, but risk estranging herself from her parents, wasn't fair.

Aaron clapped his shoulder. "I'm sure if you show up on her doorstep, she'll at least listen. She was crazy about you."

Cash was crazy about her, too, but two months had passed. Was she still? Would it matter? "It's not just us. It's her parents. They, uh…they've heard about me, and that was after they felt like I insulted them and their son's memory. They think I as good as killed him."

Silence.

Anticipation died in their expressions.

"That's heavy," Dillon said.

"Yeah." And that was it. Operation Win Back Abbi was over before it had started.

"May I intervene as a parent?" Mom came forward. "I can't put myself in Abbi's parents' place; I can only imagine how hurt and devastated they are. And to go through it a second time… Well, I don't think an apology and an explanation is ever the wrong move. They've already lost their son. But offering them your sincere feelings about their son and how much he meant to you might help them realize he wasn't alone in his last days, even if he felt alone."

Cash waited for the instant horror at the idea of confronting Daniels's parents with his failure. That emotion had faded also. Three years had passed and Cash had matured. Yeah, he could do that. "There's still my reputation." He shrugged helplessly. "I can't take it back."

He didn't even want to. He was who he was. If he were honest, he'd rather have a million one-night stands and a clean slate with respect to relationships than the baggage of several failed relationships that might hinder his openness with Abbi.

Mom spoke. "I'm proud to call you my son, and if they can't accept you, then they can suck it." Heads whipped toward her. "Well, after you discuss their son with them. Otherwise, that part of your life is your own. How you treat their daughter is between you and Abbi, but they'll still be concerned about it. All they want to know is that you'll do right by her."

"I can't imagine a family not being as proud of you as we are," Dad said.

Cash looked around at everyone. Mom was right. "The least I can do is talk with Mr. and Mrs. Daniels."

"I'll go with you for that," Dillon said. "I should've contacted them somehow, but I didn't even send a damn card."

"I don't know what to do about Abbi. I'm sure I can get her to talk to me, but I don't know if I can convince her to give me another chance."

Aaron grinned. "Well then…I think you just need to make a big enough show of your intentions to win her back."

Travis nodded and spoke in his clinical, academic tone. "You said she was trying hard to be a responsible adult, so you'll need to appeal to her wild side, prove that's the part of her you accept. Make a big show, but not just any actions will do. You need to find a way to make it about you and her, but not a stupid or empty gesture."

Cash studied the smartest man he knew. Travis had listened to him moaning over his beer about how he'd fucked it up with Abbi. Cash didn't have a wingman, he had a wingteam, and he'd be foolish not to let them do their thing.

ell, she'd made it through another week of work—almost.

Abbi leaned into the speaker. "I've included an invite card with your deposit slip. Feel free to share with family and friends." Her smile must be as empty as she felt. The customer drove away and she allowed her pleasantness to fade. New year, new attitude…that idea had lasted until 12:10 a.m. on New Year's Day. It was still the first week of January, with a long year ahead.

With a sigh, she turned to her coworker. The rest of the bank was quiet, the drive-up staying open an hour after the rest of the bank had closed.

"Fifteen minutes left," Jessica announced.

Abbi flashed another false smile. *Yay.*

"You're coming out with us tonight, right?" Jessica clapped her hands together, excited about their plans.

Abbi was less than thrilled. She had committed to a girls' night, but her heart wasn't in it—and she hadn't said when she'd go. Her coworkers had been trying to get her out after they'd found out she was single again.

I know the place you can find a nice guy, or a not so nice guy.
It's ladies' night at the Well.
How about...

Abbi wanted to scream like a banshee at them. She'd made the mistake of going out once. She'd snuck out early, feigning a headache when it had really been a heartache. How long could she sit here and wonder if Cash was doing the same thing? Had he sauntered into Barley 'n' Hops, like the ovary magnet he was, picked up a random for the night, and gone to back to her place?

Abbi couldn't fault him. The guy had opened himself up and trusted her to be his first relationship, and while he'd messed up, she'd tossed it all back into his face and walked.

The familiar icy sickness washed through her veins when she thought of him taking another chance on another woman and starting something serious. It'd been almost two and a half months. Hell, he could be engaged by now.

She massaged her temples. Why was that so much worse than one-nighter Cash?

Jessica gasped. "Oh. My. God. There's a horse in the drive-up! Oh my god, he's *hot*."

The horse was hot? Abbi spun around and her mouth dropped open. Jessica wasn't exaggerating. There was a horse in the drive-up. *Patsy Cline?* She sucked in a breath, echoing Jessica. Her gaze drifted to the man astride the horse. One hand held the reins, the other was propped on a leg, and his serious expression was focused on her.

"Cash?" she spoke and realized she hadn't used the speaker. She depressed the button. "Cash."

Patsy Cline jerked her head up and Cash murmured soothing words to her. Abbi wanted to be the one on the receiving end of his sweet whispers.

"Abbi..." He licked his lips like he was nervous—because he had a horse, at a bank, in the middle of winter. "Abbi," he started again, "dammit, I've been miserable. Tell me you've been just as miserable, too."

"You know him?" Jessica breathed. She stood right next to Abbi, staring out the window.

God, Cash looked good. The clothes he wore under his standard tan coat made her mouth quirk. Black jeans and a white button-up shirt. He'd worn his good clothes for her.

"I just want you to know how sorry I am." Hope flared in his expression, then died. "I can finally see why you were angry. You and I were a good team and I know we didn't date long, but I didn't need long to know you're the girl for me." A spark of alarm lit his gaze. "Unless you've found someone else, then Patsy Cline and I will get on along."

Jessica slapped the speaker button. "She hasn't. Totally single."

"Jessica," Abbi hissed. She slapped Jessica's hand away to talk to Cash. "Cash, you're on a damn horse in Green Bay in January."

He lifted a shoulder. "Since we're having a streak of unseasonably warm weather, the guys and I planned…this."

"Just to talk to me?"

"We thought it struck a good balance between crazy and sincere."

"They helped you plan this?"

Cash nodded solemnly. "They called me a ranching zombie on Christmas."

Abbi swallowed, her throat suddenly tight with emotion. "I think they'd call me that, too. A banking zombie."

"I would," Jessica muttered.

"I talked to your parents," he said.

Abbi's jaw dropped again.

"I explained everything about Dan—Perry. And me." He lifted a brow and gave her a pointed look. "Everything. I can't say I won them over about me, but I think they're reserving judgment until they see what you do."

"You talked to my parents?"

He ducked his head. "Me and Dillon."

Oh. She had to take a moment to process. What had they thought when Cash had shown up on their doorstep? How much did it matter to her what they thought?

Pasty Cline shifted, Cash atop her, calm as could be. Granted, they'd had a warm streak all week, but he'd driven here—with a horse. For her. And her parents. Because no matter what she told herself, it was important her parents accepted Cash. Not critical, but a deep need she wanted met.

He was here. After she'd given him a huge brush-off. Patsy Cline whinnied. Cash wouldn't risk his horse. He was being smart, and crazy, but not irresponsible—because he knew that was what she wanted.

She tapped the speaker button. "Got room for one more?"

Cash waited for Abbi to slide into the booth, then he parked himself next to her.

"Oh!" Frankie's mouth flickered like she was fighting a huge grin.

He glanced up. "I hope you don't mind I brought a friend."

"Travis's plan worked, I see." She sat across from them and her coworker loaded their table up with water and coffee.

"Barely." Abbi rolled her eyes. "I mean, he had to beg and plead, and I just felt sorry for him and gave in."

He draped an arm over the back of the booth and around Abbi's shoulders, as if he hadn't held her all weekend. Well… they'd been doin' other stuff.

"Yeah, that's why you rushed out and vaulted onto Patsy Cline's back."

"I did not vault."

"High-jumped?"

"At least I waited to put in my notice at work until after we talked."

"You were yelling as you ran out of the building."

Frankie seemed to enjoy the banter. "I know Cash said he couldn't meet last week and I wondered how it'd worked out."

Cash nodded. "I wanted to surprise you, but we were moving her down." He couldn't get Abbi out of the shit-hole she'd lived in fast enough. Her meager belongings were piled in his garage to air out the stale smoke smell.

Frankie's warm expression jumped back and forth between them. "I'm really happy you two are together."

"I won't crash every Monday," Abbi said, "but I wanted to invite you over for dinner this weekend. Whenever works for you."

Surprise crossed Frankie's expression, replaced by delight. A flash of regret popped through his mind. He'd meant to be more than a melancholy grandson every Monday morning, but he'd never gotten around to having Frankie over for anything. He hadn't been good enough company for anyone.

Frankie folded and unfolded a napkin. "Will it be just…us?"

Abbi nodded. "We'll start slow and work others in as you're more comfortable."

"We all want you around," he reassured her.

Abbi plowed forward, asking about the cats until Frankie visibly relaxed.

Before he met Abbi, it had been him. He had his cousins, his parents, Sissy, and Frankie, but ultimately, it'd been just him. But Abbi stepped into the circle with him and strengthened each and every bond to his family.

"I'm learning to ranch!" Abbi's excitement was the best belated Christmas present.

Frankie chuckled and smiled at him. "You have a good teacher."

Cash nodded. "We'd been talking about expanding the operation, and now that we have an extra body, we might as well put her to work."

Abbi's bright eyes sparkled. She ran through their unofficial plans. Cash kept her tucked in close until Frankie glanced at her watch. Her break had come to an end.

They gave her a time to show for dinner. Then Cash grasped Abbi's hand and led her out.

"What now, boss?" Abbi teased.

"I think a girl needs a horse."

Abbi stopped so suddenly, he almost ricocheted back to her. "You don't just go buy a horse."

"I know people."

"But…aren't they expensive?"

Cash ushered her to the pickup to get her out of the cold. He jogged around and climbed in. "You're working for the ranch. You need your own horse. Besides, how else are you going to ride off into the sunset with me?"

She stared at him. "I feel like you trusting me with a horse means more than anything."

It was why he was buying her the horse before the ring. He wanted her to know he had complete faith in her abilities before he proposed.

And to keep her parents from having a small heart attack at how fast they were moving.

She reached over to caress his face. "I love you, Cash."

He gripped her hand in his. "I love you, too, honey." And she'd find out how much when he gave her back the sketchbook he'd found when he was moving her out. She'd been in her bedroom packing and he'd opened it to see the drawing of him.

Right then, he'd flipped to the next page and scrawled the words he wanted her to read in exactly one month on Valentine's Day.

Marry Me.

––––––––––

After tragedy strikes his fiancée, Travis picks up the pieces of his life. But why hasn't he moved on? Don't miss Travis's story next in Guilt Ridden.

For all the latest news, sneak peeks, and BONUS content sign up for my newsletter.

Thank you for reading. I'd love to know what you thought. Please consider leaving a review of Long Hard Fall at the retailer the book was purchased from.

~Marie

ABOUT THE AUTHOR

Marie Johnston writes paranormal and contemporary romance. Before she was a writer, she was a microbiologist. Depending on the situation, she can be oddly unconcerned about germs or weirdly phobic. She's also a licensed medical technician and has worked as a public health microbiologist and as a lab tech in hospital and clinic labs. Marie's been a volunteer EMT, a college instructor, a security guard, a phlebotomist, a hotel clerk, and a coffee pourer in a bingo hall. All fodder for a writer!! She has four kids, an old cat, and a puppy that's bigger than half her kids.

mariejohnstonwriter.com
Facebook
Twitter @mjohnstonwriter

The Walker Five:
Conflict of Interest (Book 1)
Mustang Summer (Book 2)
Long Hard Fall (Book 3)
Guilt Ridden (Book 4)
Mail Order Farmer (Book 5)

www.ingramcontent.com/pod-product-compliance
Lightning Source LLC
Chambersburg PA
CBHW050356190726
48284CB00007BB/2304